I0700371

Lucky Ones

A. G. Hawkins

Copyright © 2023 by A.G.Hawkins

www.aghawkins.net

All rights reserved.

Cover Art by K.B. Barrett Designs

Editing by On the Same Page and E. Rose Books

All rights reserved.

No portion of this book may be reproduced in any form without written permission from the author, except as permitted by U.S. copyright law.

This is a work of fiction. Names, characters, places, and incidents either are the product of the author's imagination or are used fictitiously. Any resemblance to actual persons, living or dead, events, or locales is entirely coincidental.

For those pursuing their dreams,
and for those who need a little push

Author's Note

Dear Readers,

When you read my stories, I hope to write relatable characters. My characters go through situations, sometimes dark. For a list of what tropes or types of content you may see within this story or any of my others, you can visit my website at aghawkins.net.

Thank you,

A. G. Hawkins

CHAPTER ONE

S he stared off into the distance, her body feeling numb. This happened on occasion; disconnecting from everything around her.

"You better not be canceling on me," Vanessa's sister said through their FaceTime call, forcing her out of her trance.

Vanessa shook herself out of her daze and glanced down at her phone, propped up in front of her bathroom mirror. She lifted her make-up brush and attempted to add some color to her cheeks. She hadn't worn much makeup in the past six months, and she felt a bit rusty at doing herself all up.

"I'm not," Vanessa said. "I'm getting ready. I was just going to ask if you'd do my hair."

"Oh, sure," Bradley answered. Vanessa looked at her phone to see her sister's raven hair drawn to one side, her purple balayage taking center stage. Unlike her sister, Vanessa never felt brave enough to dye her hair. She kept it its natural dirty blonde, which had dulled in the past few months.

"I just don't know what to do with it, and *you* are the one who is forcing me to go to this thing."

"It's a birthday dinner for Addison. You know, my best friend since I was 3? You act like I'm forcing you on a blind date," Bradley said with a scoff.

The thought of any type of dating made a shiver run up Vanessa's spine. She finished her make-up and decided it was good enough before lifting her phone to get a better view of her sister.

"You look good," Bradley said.

Even though over the years her sister had toned down some, Bradley still stood out when the two of them stood by one another. She wore a tank-style top that showed off her dragon tattoo on her shoulder, and every one of her ear piercings held an earring in it.

"So do you. I'll be over in about ten minutes to your place."

"Okay."

Vanessa mussed her hair once more before deciding it would be best to let her sister deal with it. She was much better at these types of things. She still couldn't believe she was going to this party tonight, but it had been the only way to get Bradley off her back.

She grabbed her purse and walked out of her home. When she got into her car, her phone rang. Even though she couldn't see who was calling, she knew who it was: Grey. Her heart skipped a beat, like it always did when he called.

She lifted the phone, not intending on answering. Then she hit the button to send it to voicemail. Instead of leaving her a voicemail, a text came up on her screen.

I know you're not talking to me. I just wanted to let you know that I've moved on like you asked. I found someone. Her name is Emma. I felt you should hear it from me.

She read over the words twice, the heartache causing her free hand to whiten as it clutched against the steering wheel. A picture popped up of the two of them. Grey and his new girlfriend, Emma.

Vanessa stared at the picture for a few seconds while she attempted to calm her breathing. Emma's arm was intertwined with Grey's, and both were smiling brightly. She was beautiful; he was gorgeous. They were the perfect pair.

Good, Vanessa typed back, deciding it was best to respond to show him that this was what she wanted. *I'm happy for you, Grey, truly.*

She left it at that, turning her phone on silent to forget about it, and driving to her sister's apartment. She parked in the parking lot and made her way quickly up the stairs. Then she knocked on the door. Her sister answered almost immediately.

"Come on in!"

Vanessa opened the door.

"You should keep your door locked," Vanessa said.

"It usually is. I unlocked it because I knew you were coming over." Bradley sat on her bed. Her apartment was a studio with everything in one large room. It was a bit unconventional for Vanessa, but it worked for her sister.

"What time do we have to be at the restaurant?" Vanessa checked the time on her watch.

"Not for another hour, so plenty of time to do your hair. Now, come on and sit down."

"To the birthday girl!" they all called out. Bradley clinked her drink with everyone else and looked at her sister who sat beside her, staying quiet and withdrawn from the group.

"You're having fun?" she whispered.

"Yeah."

Bradley frowned. She saw the tremor in Vanessa's hand; a tremor that seemed nearly permanent lately. Her sister had always been straight and narrow, overwhelmed by these types of events. But over the past few months, it became more than that. She looked on edge at every turn, almost like a wild animal afraid she would be attacked.

"Addison said something about going to the bar down the street. Are you game?"

Vanessa's cheeks sunk in slightly, but she nodded.

"Sure. Sounds fun."

"You're really forcing, this aren't you? Trying to prove to me that you're okay?"

"I don't know what you're talking about. I am okay. Why wouldn't I be?" Vanessa challenged back.

Bradley bit her tongue.

They paid their tab and exited the restaurant to go to the bar down the street. It was part of an old, brick building with a bright green neon sign up front.

"Lucky Ones," Bradley mused. "Interesting name for a bar. Are there rainbows and leprechauns inside?" she playfully said, nudging Vanessa's shoulder.

"I don't know. I've never been," Vanessa murmured.

With a sigh, Bradley returned her attention to the group. It had already died down, and now there were only a few of them. They entered the small bar in Savannah, Georgia. Instead of any sort of St. Patrick's theme, there was no theme outside of the few random pictures hung on the brick walls. Despite that, the bar was crowded, and they had to force their way up to the bar to order.

"Um," Bradley said when their time came. "A soda for me, and my sister, Vanessa, will have water, right?"

"Sure."

"That's all?" the bartender asked, incredulous.

"Not drinking this late, I have work tomorrow," Bradley explained. She smiled at him, completely overtaken by how hot he was. He had a pepper and salt beard, toned arms with tattoos, and the most gorgeous eyes.

"Fine." He turned away to make their drinks.

"God, he's fine," Bradley said. Her sister just shook her head, not impressed with Bradley's taste in men. "Sorry he's not some genius with a bland personality."

"Grey is not bland," Vanessa bit. She grabbed her water the moment it was set down on the bar and turned away.

"Shit," Bradley murmured under her breath. She rushed after her sister. "I didn't mean it like that. Grey is awesome. I like him a lot, but you did break up with him."

"I know," Vanessa said. "And he's moved on, so it's all good."

"Wait, what? What do you mean he's moved on?"

Vanessa dug her phone out of her purse and showed Bradley the picture of him and his new girlfriend. Bradley grabbed the phone from her sister and scrutinized the new couple.

"Oh shit!"

"Why do you insist on cursing all the time?" Vanessa said. "And it's fine. This is what I wanted."

"But is it?" Bradley asked. "I think if you'd just tell him—"

"There's nothing to tell." Vanessa took her phone back before she turned her wrist to look at the time on her watch. "It's late. I think I'm going to head back home. Can you grab a ride with someone else, or do you want to leave now?"

"I'll grab a ride. Be safe and text me when you get home." She kissed her sister's cheek and gave her upper arm a squeeze.

Bradley watched her sister exit the bar before making her way toward her friends. As she did, she bumped into another customer. Her drink fell from her hands, but the stranger caught it before it could spill and break all over the floor.

"Close call," the man said.

"Yeah." Bradley smiled up at him. He was good looking with piercing black eyes. "You saved the day."

"I spilled some of your drink. Why don't you let me buy you another?"

Bradley glanced over his shoulder at the birthday party. They wouldn't miss her if she didn't head back that way. Her apartment was only a few blocks from here, so she could walk home if she had to.

"Sure."

Bradley took a seat at the table the man had already procured.

"Just a soda?"

"Yes, please."

The man walked back up to the bar. While he was away, Bradley got a message from Addison, who said they decided they wanted to try somewhere else instead. She texted back, saying that she would stay here. Right as she was putting her phone back, she saw the man sitting down beside her with both drinks.

"I'm Allen," he introduced himself.

"Bradley."

The room felt unsteady. Bradley placed her hands on the edge of the table, wondering how she felt so woozy when her last beer was hours ago.

"Woah there," Allen said, placing his hand on her back. "Are you okay?"

"Yeah," she slurred. She tried to look around, but her vision was blurry. She closed her eyes and reopened them in an attempt to steady her eyesight.

"Perhaps, I should walk you home."

Bradley nodded—or at least, she thought she did. She was struggling. Her mind attempted to make sense of what was happening to her, but she didn't know up from down at the moment.

"Maybe I should sit." She tried to sit back down, but she felt Allen's hands on her back, trying to push her toward the door.

"You'll feel better when you're home," he said into her ear.

"But my sister. I should call my sister."

Allen shoved her, preventing her from reaching for her phone in her pocket.

"You need to lay down. Come on."

Jones did his regular ten-minute scan of his bar. As his eyes scanned over his guests, he saw a woman leaning against a man who was pushing her roughly. The hairs on the back of his neck stood up, and he quickly made his way over to the two of them.

When he reached the couple, he noticed the woman right away. She'd come in just a little bit earlier and had ordered a soda with her sister. She hadn't been drinking.

"My date got a little too drunk," the man said with a smirk. "Don't worry, I'll get her out of here before she makes a scene."

"You're not her date," Jones countered. "She came in with a bunch of women."

"Yeah, but then she sat down with me for a drink, so, my date."

Jones eyed the woman next to the man. She could hardly keep her head up and looked as though she might pass out at any minute.

"Ma'am, do you know this man?"

The woman looked up.

"My sister…" she slurred.

"You're not leaving with her," Jones said. The man glanced at the door, back to Jones, and then down at the woman. He dropped his hold on her, forcing Jones to reach out to keep her from falling to the ground.

By the time he had a hold on her, he noticed the guy running out of the building.

"Go, get him!" he yelled at two of his bouncers. They ran out to follow him. As he lifted the woman up into his arms, he noticed that the rest of the guests for the night had quieted to try and figure out what was going on. All eyes were on him. "Everything is fine," he lied.

He heard more commotion around him, but ignored it. For now, he needed to find somewhere to put the woman safely. He walked the woman over to an empty booth, setting her down.

"He disappeared, boss," Mads said, walking over to him.

"Well, we need to call 911. I think he's drugged her. Call for an ambulance and the police. I'm going to try and find her phone."

"Why?"

"She asked for her sister, and if I remember correctly, her sister's name is Vanessa."

He saw a small bag over her arm and gently looked inside, glad to find a phone without any sort of passcode. He found the sister's name. Thankfully, there was only one Vanessa. He dialed it.

"Are you stuck?" an annoyed voice said on the other end. "You didn't get drunk, did you? You know it's nearly one a.m., don't you?"

"Um, is this Vanessa?" Jones asked.

"Who is this? Why do you have my sister's phone?"

"I'm Jones, from the bar. Your sister appears to have been drugged."

Chapter Two

R ed, bright lights ran past her as Vanessa attempted to find a place to park at the hospital. She groaned before turning into the parking garage. Luckily, she found a place to park right by the exit. She hated parking in parking garages alone as a woman, especially at night.

Once she got out of her car, she grabbed her phone. Jones had given her his number and had been updating her on what was going on with her sister. The last thing he sent was that her sister was in the ER.

"May I help you?" the man at the front desk asked.

"My sister, Bradley Price, was brought in. The bartender said she was drugged."

"Oh, yes, she was just brought in. She's right around the corner. I'll have a nurse take you back."

A nurse came over and began to walk Vanessa back to where her sister was. Before they reached her, Vanessa caught sight of

Jones, standing alone against a wall. He had his foot propped up behind him and his head bent down, looking at his phone.

"Jones!" Vanessa called out. He looked up, recognizing her immediately. Then he pushed himself off the wall to stand up fully. He was a good half-foot taller than her.

"Ah, Vanessa."

"Thank you for saving Bradley," Vanessa said, sincerely. "Who knows what would have happened if you hadn't stopped him."

"No need to thank me. I'm just glad she's all right. I'll leave now that you're here."

There was so much more Vanessa knew she should say, but she just gave him a nod and let him go back to his work. The nurse pointed to a curtain where her sister was, leaving her alone in the middle of the small hallway. There were beeps and random sounds going on around her, making her feel sick. She hated hospitals.

With a deep breath, she pushed back her fears and widened the curtain. Her sister was passed out on the bed. There was an IV in her arm. As terrifying as this all was, Vanessa was so glad her sister hadn't been harmed any more than this. It could have been worse. So much worse.

She pulled a chair closer to her sister and took Bradley's hand into her own. Her thumb stroked over the stars tattoo on her sister's wrist as she blinked back the tears.

"Ms. Price?" Vanessa turned to see a woman in scrubs and a white jacket, holding a clipboard.

"Yes?"

"Your sister's test results have come back."

"So was she drugged?"

"Yes, we found rohypnol in her bloodwork. The good news is she should be just fine after it clears her system. She'll feel a bit groggy when she wakes up, maybe a headache or some nausea. We'll watch her for the next several hours."

"But she'll be all right? The guy didn't hurt her?"

"No, Mr. Jones stepped in before anything could happen to her."

Vanessa let out a grateful sigh. She held Bradley's hand a bit tighter, feeling protective of her little sister.

"Thank you, doctor."

Bright lights accosted her eyes the moment she tried to open them. She turned her head, moaning. Her head pounded. As she tried to pull her hand up to rub against her temple, she felt resistance.

"Bradley?"

What was her sister doing in her bedroom? And why was it so bright?

"Bradley?"

"Can we turn off the lights?" Bradley croaked.

"Sadly, I can't. There's not a light switch in here."

Bradley opened her eyes wider to find her sister sitting in front of her. Her dirty blonde hair was in a messy bun, and she still wore the same makeup from the night before, though it was smudged around her eyes.

"Where am I?"

"The hospital," Vanessa said with a yawn.

"What?" She sat up too quickly, pressing her hand against her forehead.

"Take it easy. You were drugged last night at the bar. Jones, the owner, happened to see the guy trying to leave with you. He stopped him and called an ambulance."

Bradley tried to process what her sister was telling her. Drugged? Man? The last thing she remembered was being at the bar with Vanessa. But then another memory came over her and she remembered the guy with the dark eyes. Allen. His name had been Allen.

"Lay back down," Vanessa ordered. Bradley allowed her sister to gently push her back against the pillows.

"Oh shit!" Bradley called out.

"Language!"

Bradley rolled her eyes.

"What time is it?"

"Um, almost eleven."

"Shit! I've missed my shift at work. If I leave now, I'll be about…three hours late. Shit!" Bradley attempted to climb out of the bed again, but her sister held down her shoulder firmly.

"You're not leaving the hospital. They're still monitoring you. Plus, I already called your work and told them you were here. Now, lay back down." Her sister's authoritative voice had a calming effect on her, and Bradley settled back in the bed.

"You always make sure I'm taken care of."

"Well, of course, I do. I'm your sister. Are you hungry? I can go see if I can find someone to grab you some food." Vanessa stood, ready to do whatever Bradley asked of her. She'd always been a mama hen to Bradley.

"No, I couldn't eat right now. My stomach is unsettled." Bradley didn't miss the way her sister's eyes darkened in recognition. "Was that how it was for you?"

"I don't know what you're talking about," Vanessa said, brushing it off. "Now let me figure out where that nurse went." Vanessa went over to where the curtain was to peek out. Then she turned back to Bradley and gave her a sheepish smile. "Oh, and Mom and Dad should be here soon."

"You called them?"

"I had to. You're in the hospital."

Bradley groaned. The very last thing she wanted after being drugged by some random perp was a visit from her parents at the hospital.

"Could you just shoot me instead?"

"Oh Bradley." Her sister disappeared behind the curtain, off in search of someone.

While she was left alone, Bradley searched for her phone. She saw her purse hanging on the side of a chair. She sat herself up and drew the covers off of her. She still wore her clothes from the previous night, her tank top and mini skirt. Her parents would have a field day over the outfit. She wished they'd put her in one of those awful hospital gowns while she was asleep.

She reached for her purse and dug out her phone. It was nearly dead, but she saw several messages from her boss at work.

Your sister called. You will be here at some point today, right?

This is ridiculous. Call me.

If you're not in by noon, don't expect to come back.

Bradley sunk down on the edge of the bed. It was already ten forty-five. She wouldn't make it in time. She dialed the number.

"There you are. Please tell me you're on your way," her boss said.

"I'm not. I'm still at the hospital. Didn't my sister call you?" Bradley asked.

"Bradley, I've heard all the excuses in the book," her boss replied haughtily.

"But I am actually in the hospital. I can have the doctor call you."

"Just forget it. I had Diana come in for your shift. Don't come back."

"But—"

The phone line ended. Bradley's stomach sank. She lost her job at the department store.

"I couldn't find anyone," Vanessa said, entering the room. "Well, I did find someone with Jell-O and grabbed cherry, your favorite." Vanessa nearly shoved the Jell-O into Bradley's hands. "You should eat."

"I lost my job," Bradley said, her eyes staring at the bright red concoction in her hands.

"What do you mean you lost your job? I spoke to your manager. I explained what happened. She said she understood."

"Yeah, well, she lied. I've never missed a day of work before. I've worked there for three years." Bradley muttered. What would she do now?

"Let me call her."

Bradley placed her phone beside her where her sister couldn't reach.

"Absolutely not. It's fine. I'll find another job."

"You lost your job?"

As if her day couldn't get any worse, her mother stepped into the room, quickly followed behind by her father. Her mother's eyes ran over her frame, and she made a disapproving sound with a clearing of her throat.

"Why don't we all sit down," Vanessa said, stepping in as the moderator between Bradley and their parents. "Bradley should still be taking it easy. She's been through a lot."

"So some guy drugged you? Have you pressed charges?" her father asked.

"And are you sure you didn't accept the drugs?" Her mother kept looking at the tattoo on her shoulder.

"I don't do drugs," Bradley said. "And no, I haven't pressed charges yet. But I will."

"The bartender saved her. It could have been much worse." Vanessa sat down next to Bradley on the bed. "I saw him earlier and thanked him."

"I just don't understand how it could have happened. Why were you even at the bar?" her mother asked.

"We were at a birthday party," Vanessa said, answering for her. "I had to leave early, but Bradley had a safe ride home."

Bradley rested her head on her sister's shoulder. She felt woozy, and this conversation with her parents was not helping.

"Perhaps next time you should wear something less revealing," her father suggested.

"Okay." Vanessa shot up, nearly making Bradley fall over. "I don't think the doctors want there to be too many people in this little space, since she doesn't have a real room. I can stay with her until she's discharged." She helped their parents out of their chairs and nearly shoved them out of the small, curtained area.

Bradley could hear them chatting on the other side, but she was glad she didn't have to deal with them. Just a moment later, Vanessa came back around and sat back down.

"Thank you," Bradley said.

"I never should have called them."

"You had to. They never would have forgiven you if you hadn't."

"I am really glad you're okay," Vanessa said, reaching out to take Bradley's hands within her own. "Really glad."

"Me too."

"Here are some pamphlets," a nurse told Bradley at discharge.

"What for?" Bradley took them, confused.

"Well, I'm sure after what happened you may have some questions or some feelings you aren't sure how to deal with. These pamphlets may help answer those questions. They also have numbers you can call if you need someone to speak to."

Bradley looked at the top pamphlet. There was a grainy photo of a girl crying on it. Beneath her, it said, *Feeling vulnerable? Reach out.*

"Yeah, I don't need these," Bradley said. She attempted to hand them back to the nurse. "I feel just fine." But before she could give them back, her sister snatched them out of her hands.

"Thank you. I'll hold them for her."

The nurse made a displeased sound, but didn't say anything else. Bradley had already signed the discharge papers, so she could finally go home and try to figure out what she was going to do about her job situation. She did not have time to dwell on what had happened. Plus, nothing *had* happened. The bartender had stepped in and saved the day.

"You might need these later," Vanessa explained. She placed them into her own purse. Bradley met her eyes. "What? You might. You haven't had time to process what that man did to you, or could have done."

Bradley scoffed.

"What?" Vanessa asked.

"You're lecturing me on facing what happened when you won't be honest with yourself about what happened to you six months ago."

Vanessa's face paled before turning beet red with a flush of anger.

"Stop it," she said. "You have no idea what happened; you are completely off on the whole subject matter. Just stop."

Bradley, who was normally the more competitive sibling, knew her sister's limits. Right now was not the time to push this. She sighed.

"You're right. I'm sorry. Now, can you please drive me home?"

Vanessa drove her sister back to her studio apartment in silence. Her mind swirled with thoughts and memories she didn't want to face. She dug her hands tighter around the steering wheel, glad to see her sister's parking lot up ahead.

"You know Mom and Dad love you, right?" Vanessa asked her sister as she parked the car. "They're just..."

"Difficult?"

"Well," Vanessa laughed, "yes."

"It's fine," Bradley said, unbothered. "I learned a long time ago that I'm the screw up and you're the perfect one."

"I'm not—"

"Vanessa, I'd much rather be seen as the screw up. You're the one with all the pressure put on you. I get to just do my thing, because it doesn't matter what I do. They won't be impressed either way."

"I think you're pretty awesome," she said, sincerely.

"I think you are, too." Bradley reached over and pulled her sister into a hug. Vanessa held her sister tightly. "Thanks for coming the moment I needed you."

"I always will."

Vanessa let go of her sister and watched her enter her apartment building. Once she was sure her sister was safe, she went back home. She would have to get some of her work done from home.

She'd worked for the insurance company for nearly ten years now, since she graduated college. It was a nice, corporate job with nice, corporate pay. She'd worked herself up the ladder and was close to her next promotion.

When she entered the house, she went straight to her office to get to work. She opened up her computer, but ended up on her social media site instead. Her curser lingered over Grey's name. She clicked on it to see his page. Since their break up, she'd avoided all forms of social media. But now, she wanted to know more about what he was up to, and more importantly, who this *Emma* was.

He loved posting on social media. Over the course of just the last month, there were several photos he'd posted with Emma tagged in them. Her eyes lingered on Grey, who smiled brightly in every photo with Emma, his hazel eyes lit up with joy.

He was happy.

Vanessa stared at the latest post for a good minute, her eyes unable to leave Grey's happy face. She felt an overwhelming wave of sadness sweep over her. But she couldn't cry. She'd done this to herself.

Instead, she closed out the page and went back to focusing on her work.

Chapter Three

There were no job prospects. Bradley tried talking to her manager again, and even went up to the job site, only to be turned away. No one else was hiring—at least no one who would pay her a living wage. If she couldn't find a job, she'd have to move back home. That was not an option.

She opened up her laptop and checked her bank account. She had just enough money to survive for one more month. At least that gave her some time before she would be forced to ask her parents for help.

She could hear them now.

If you'd gone to college and gotten a good job like your sister, you wouldn't be here.

Maybe you should stop wearing all those earrings and dye your hair back to its natural color.

Just thinking about it made Bradley groan. She slid off her bed and placed her laptop back on her small desk.

Every so often, her phone would ding with another message from one of her friends. Through the grapevine, they'd all heard what happened at the bar. Several had issued apologies for leaving her there alone.

Can I take you to lunch? the latest message from Addison asked.

Not today, but maybe later this week?
Sure.
Bradley knew she should be resting, but she felt antsy. She hardly stayed in her apartment unless she was getting ready or sleeping. Normally, she was working or out with friends. She wasn't sure what to do with all of this free time. She slid on her shoes, grabbed her keys, and decided she was going to go out. Maybe along the way, she'd also find a job.

While the lunchtime rush was his least favorite time of day, Jones had to admit that his customers always tipped his staff well. He stood behind the bar, wiping it down before the nighttime rush came in.

He glanced up at the door to see a woman he recognized standing outside. Her hair was pulled back off of her face and she wore jeans with a leather jacket. She stood at the door and grabbed the handle momentarily before walking away. Then she repeated this twice, making Jones laugh. He stepped around the counter and to the front door, opening it.

She paused with her hand reached out to the door.

"Vanessa," Jones said.

"Sorry. I…" She chewed on the edge of her lip. "I just wanted to thank you for saving my sister."

"Come on in," Jones offered. He widened the door and motioned for her to join him. She cautiously stepped into the building, tucking a stray hair behind her ear. "Would you like something to drink?"

"Um, no that's alright. I really only came here to say thank you."

"Don't worry about it. All I did was the bare minimum. I'm glad your sister is okay."

"Oh, me too." Vanessa rubbed her hands nervously in front of her. "I just keep thinking what else could have happened." Her body shook.

"Are you sure you don't want anything? I could have Mads fix you up a burger really fast."

"No. I'm fine. I ate before I came." She continued to search around her, looking as though at any moment someone might jump out to grab her. He'd never met someone who appeared so on edge. "Well, thank you. I feel I should do more—"

"You don't need to. Honestly."

"Well, thanks, again. I should probably leave," Vanessa said.

He walked her to the door. She glanced up at him, giving him a small smile before walking away. Before he could close the door, he saw Bradley coming up on the other side of the pebbled street.

"Is this the sister thank-you tour?" he asked.

Bradley cocked up her eyebrow.

"What?"

"Your sister was just here. She left." He pointed in the direction Vanessa went.

"What?" Her eyes searched for her sister, but she'd just missed her. "Well, I guess she had the same idea as me. I've come to thank you."

She placed her thumbs in the belt loops of her worn out jeans and swayed on her thick, dark boots.

"No thanks necessary, just as I told your sister."

"Well, you saved my life, so I should thank you," Bradley insisted.

"Why don't you come inside? I'll get you a burger."

"Okay."

Bradley stepped inside the bar and took a seat up on one of the stools. He grabbed her a bottle of water.

"Sealed," he told her.

"Yeah, I guess I will be a bit more worried about my drinks now. You know, I've always been really cautious. I guess I let my guard down last night. I can't believe I did that," Bradley said, scratching the back of her neck.

"You're not to blame. He is." Jones called back for Mads to make a cheeseburger. "But you're alright? The doctors gave you a clear bill of health?"

"Yep. Clean, and healthy as a whistle."

Jones grinned, pleased. She had been his first—and hopefully only—drugged customer that he had to rush to the hospital. He'd sent off plenty of creeps, though. It was the downside of owning a bar.

"So, Vanessa is your sister?"

"Yes, my older sister. Why?"

"I don't know. You both seem so different," Jones said.

"We are. We have sweet Vanessa and edgy Bradley," she said playfully.

"So, did you give yourself an edgy name? Or?"

"Bradley is edgy?" Bradley chuckled. "No, this name is on my birth certificate. My grandmother's maiden name was Bradley, so my parents always said they'd name their son Bradley. When my mom had me, it nearly killed her. She had to have a C-section and a hysterectomy, so I was their last kid. They had to use the name on me. I've been the disappointment since day one."

"I doubt that."

"Eh." Bradley shrugged. "What about you? What kind of name is Jones?"

"It's my last name," Jones answered. He inhaled sharply, knowing what question would come next. Everyone was always so nosey.

"What's your first?"

"Oh, yeah, you don't get to know that."

"I don't? Why, is it some weird name?" Bradley eyed him carefully. Mads brought her food out and slid it toward Bradley. She began munching on a fry. "Bartholomew?"

"No, that is not my name. And what my name is doesn't matter. I go by Jones. Have since I was ten."

"Ten?" Bradley wrinkled her nose. "Your name must be really bad then."

"It's not."

Jones never liked his name. After his mother died, he decided he wouldn't be called by it anymore. She had been the only person he didn't mind calling him by it.

The two of them fell into a comfortable silence. Jones worked on organizing behind the bar to prepare for the upcoming evening. When Bradley finished her burger, she stood.

"Well, Jones, thanks again for saving my life. Thanks for the food, too."

"Not a problem."

Bradley gave him a nod. She headed toward the door, but paused when she caught sight of something, turning back to face Jones.

"You're hiring?"

"Hmm?"

"You're hiring? There's a help wanted sign on the window."

"Oh, yeah. Need a bartender," Jones answered.

"And what does that pay look like?"

"You bartend?" He stared at her suspiciously.

"I do whatever brings me money," she answered with a laugh. "But yes, I can bartend. I lost my job because I was in the hospital last night. I *really* need a new job."

"They fired you?"

"Yep." Bradley stepped closer to him. "What do you say? Give me a shot? I could come in tonight, show you I can handle it."

He looked her over. She was a tiny thing. He doubted she could lift half the bottles of alcohol, much less make several drinks in a short time period under pressure. However, he knew not to judge a book by its cover.

"Sure, why not. But wait until tomorrow. You probably should rest."

"You sound just like my sister. But okay. See you tomorrow. What time?"

"Seven."

"Perfect."

"You're working there now?" Vanessa adjusted the phone on her ear. She placed her frozen meal into the microwave and hit the buttons for it to cook.

"Sort of. I have a trial run tomorrow night," Bradley answered.

"Do you know how to bartend? You aren't much of a drinker."

"I bartended for two years at that dive over on Tybee," Bradley reminded her.

"Oh right, I forgot." Vanessa went over to sit on her couch and turned on the television, keeping the sound on low.

"He told me you also went by today to tell him thank you."

"I did." Vanessa scanned through the channels, trying to decide something to watch. "I guess you and I just missed one another." She finally settled on a cooking show right as her microwave beeped, letting her know that her chicken pot pie was done.

"We did."

"And you're feeling better?" Vanessa asked as she got up to go and get her food.

"I feel fine."

"Ow!" Vanessa nearly burnt her finger when she pulled out her food.

"Are you okay?"

"Yes, it's just my dinner. I burned myself." She sucked her finger into her mouth in an attempt to ease the pain.

"Oh."

The line went quiet for a moment, which gave Vanessa a chance to get her food onto a plate and grab a fork. She walked back over to her couch and sunk down.

"So, are you excited about this new job?" Vanessa asked.

"Sure, it's a job," Bradley said simply. "It'll be something different. I was getting bored at the department store. Same thing every day. Lucky Ones should be more interesting."

"Yeah." Vanessa blew on her food to take a small bite. "Just be safe." To be honest, Vanessa worried about her sister working in a bar late at night. There were too many creeps out there in this world. But there was some comfort in knowing Jones would be there with her to keep an eye out for those creeps.

"I will be."

Ding.

Bradley glanced down at her phone and saw a text from Addison. In the text, there was a link. She clicked on it.

The Lucky One?

After several women have been found sexually assaulted and left behind the bars they were drugged in, the case may finally have a lead. Bradley Price may have been the next victim, had she not been saved by the owner of Lucky Ones.

"How do they know my name?" she asked herself, shocked. She scanned over the rest of the article, seeing what else was said about her and the man who'd drugged her. There wasn't much else. However, below the article were comments. Someone had posted a picture of her.

Look how she dresses. Are we surprised?

How do we know she's even telling the truth?

As if, she's not even that pretty. I'm sure if someone wanted to drug girls, they wouldn't have chosen her.

Bradley closed out of the article, feeling gross.

You're famous. Addison's next message came through. *Your name is everywhere. I even saw you on the news!*

Great.

A moment later, the phone rang.

"Yes, Mom?"

"You're on the news."

"What?" Bradley played dumb. She knew her mother would try to make this into a much bigger deal than it was. Though, despite thinking that way, her stomach twisted as she thought about her name and this story being out there for everyone to see.

"Yes, on tonight's news. They think the guy who drugged you is some serial rapist. Perhaps you should come and sleep at our house until they find him."

"Mom, he's not going to come after me," Bradley said, rolling her eyes.

"How do you know that?"

"It doesn't feel like coming after victims is his M.O. I should be safe."

She heard her father calling to her mother.

"See, your father says you should come to the house."

"I can't. I have a new job."

"Oh?"

"Yes. Oh, I have to go. My food is here." She told her mother goodbye and hung up the phone before they could try to ask her any more questions.

She searched for her name in Google and was surprised to see many local news sites writing about what happened. She clicked on a few of them, but they all said the same few things. It was disconcerting. And she had to admit, it made her feel unsafe. What if her parents were right, and this Allen guy did come after her?

She called her sister back.

"I'm in the news," Bradley said. "What happened is plastered all over the local news. How messed up is that?"

"What? Why would they do that?"

"Seems this is a pattern. Lots of girls have been found behind bars, drugged and raped. I was the lucky one to escape him," Bradley told her as she tried to keep her mind from imagining what could have happened had Allen not been stopped.

"Do you want to sleep here tonight?"

Bradley sighed in relief.

"You wouldn't mind?"

"No. Come on over."

Vanessa opened her garage for her sister to come inside. She took her sister's small, overnight bag from her shoulder and handed her a bowl of chocolate ice cream.

"Thanks," Bradley said.

"No problem."

Vanessa went to take Bradley's bag into the guest room and then came back out to sit with Bradley on the couch. She tried to remember the last time they'd had a sleep over with one another.

"Don't tell Mom and Dad I slept over and was scared," Bradley said. "They told me to come to their house, and I told them I was fine."

"I wouldn't dare," Vanessa told her with a wink. They both grinned, knowing how their parents could be. They were always keeping one another's secrets. Vanessa knew Bradley was the only other person in the world that knew all of hers, and that it was likely the same for her. "Want to watch a movie?"

"Aren't you exhausted? You were at the hospital all night with me and you have to work tomorrow," Bradley said.

Vanessa picked at the edge of her sleeve and shrugged her shoulders.

"I don't really sleep much anyway."

Vanessa didn't miss the way the corner of her sister's mouth curled down and into a frown. She leaned closer to Vanessa, a worried expression on her face. Her mouth opened and Vanessa felt herself preparing a response to whatever her sister said. However, Bradley shook her head and sat back, deciding not to say anything.

Vanessa felt her body relax and she lifted her remote.

"What movie do you want to watch?" she asked.

"Something funny."

They found something to watch on one of the streaming services. As the movie started, Vanessa curled up onto her couch near her sister, and before she knew it, she fell asleep.

CHAPTER FOUR

J ones was in the middle of finding something to put on the televisions for the guests when he heard the front door bell ring. He turned, surprised to see Bradley already here for the evening. His eyes glanced at the clock, which said six fifteen. It was a good first step.

Bradley walked into the nearly empty bar and bounced up onto one of the stools before looking around the place.

"So, what time does it start picking up?" She tugged the edge of her ponytail and clucked her tongue.

"It's Monday, so we have a little rush from 8 to 10, but that's about it on weeknights. Otherwise, it's pretty tame," he told her. He looked her up and down as she remained sitting on the barstool. "Well, are you ready to work?"

"Of course I am." Bradley jumped off the stool. Even though she was small, she had this energy about her that made her seem like she was taking up a ton of space. She walked around to the other side of the bar and placed her hands on the counter. "What should I do first?"

"Clean up the bar, and organize everything in preparation for the next order. When customers come in, you'll take both their food and drink orders if they are sitting at the bar. I'll shadow you for a few days to help you grow accustomed to everything," Jones explained. "You can make drinks, can't you?"

"Yes," Bradley said, giving him a bright smile. "I worked at a bar for two years. I know the ins and outs of it all."

"Good," Jones said. He took her through the basics of the bar and his rules about how things should be kept. He also went over his expectations; his biggest being that they I.D. everyone who asks for a drink.

"I don't care if they look one hundred, I.D. them."

"Will do."

"I'm serious," he added.

"I believe you," Bradley said back.

The door dinged again, letting him know he had more customers for the evening. They headed to the booth over at the corner. He left Bradley alone at the bar and went to take their orders, deciding he'd wait to add that to Bradley's plate until she grew more comfortable behind the counter.

When he returned, he found her grabbing a beer for a customer and handing it to him. The man walked away, leaving the two of them alone.

"His name was Samson. Is that your name?" she asked.

"No," Jones said, grumbling beneath his breath. What was it with this girl and her obsession about what his name was?

"When will you tell me what it is?" Bradley asked. She bounced on her heels, grinning up at him. Her ponytail moved side to side as she moved up and down.

"Never."

"Why? Is it Ebenezer?"

"No."

"Oh! Is it super religious, like Jedidiah?"

"No. Now, stop guessing. There are more customers coming in."

She should be at home getting ready for bed; not out—especially not at a bar. Vanessa glanced up at the sign and reminded herself she was just being a big sister, checking in on her sister's first day at her new job.

When she walked inside, it was less crowded than the other night, but still full. The people all around made her nervous, but she forced herself to keep moving forward. There had been a time in her life when she, Vanessa Price, hadn't been scared of anything.

Between the flow of people walking around, she saw her sister behind the bar with a bright smile on her face. She was chatting with everyone as she fixed their drinks. Vanessa wasn't surprised. Her sister always knew how to get along with people.

"Ness!"

Vanessa smiled and made her way through the crowd to the bar. Her sister made a cup of water and handed it to her.

"It's nearly ten at night," Bradley said, surprised.

"I know. I wanted to give you time to settle in before coming to see how it was going, and it looks like it's going well."

"It is."

Bradley got pulled away by another customer, so Vanessa sat down on one of the stools. She took a small sip of her drink before placing her hand over the top. In the past six months, she hadn't touched any alcohol and she only drank water, but it didn't keep her from making sure the tops of her drinks were always covered if anyone else was around.

She took in all of the bar. The other night when she was inside, she hadn't paid much attention to it. It was just another bar on a street of bars. But tonight, she took in the bland walls and random pictures hanging up. There wasn't much style to the place, with random barstools that didn't match any of the tables. Yet, it seemed no one cared, because it was packed. Even before *everything*, she'd never been too keen of being in a tight space where people were loud and drinking around her.

"Sorry about that." Bradley was back over next to her.

"Nothing to apologize for, you're at work. You don't need to entertain me. I only came to support you," Vanessa said right as Bradley was pulled away again. She took a sip of her drink and thought about how she could have invited someone to come with her. But who? Most of her friends had also been Grey's friends, and she'd stopped returning messages from her other friends after she messed everything up. For the past six months, the only constants in her life were her job, her sister, and her parents. She had let everything else fade away.

As she watched her sister work, Vanessa sat there. She knew she should order something to eat and not just take a space at the bar, but it was late and she wasn't hungry. She sat there for a few more minutes before deciding she'd been there long enough. She tried to get her sister's attention, but Bradley was busy. Instead, she placed a twenty-dollar bill in the tip jar and left.

Like he did every night after closing, Jones counted the money from the tip jar, bundling it up into sections for everyone except himself. For a Monday, they'd done better in tips than normal. He wondered if Bradley was behind that. She was the first woman to work here in several years.

"Here," he said, handing her the bundle of money. "Good job."

"So, I have a job?" She brought her hand up to her ear, showing off the stars along her wrist.

"Well, it's still not official," Jones said carefully, "but I'd say the odds are good."

"Yes!" Bradley clapped her hands together. "You won't regret it. I'm a great worker. Never missed a day, except when I was drugged, at my last job."

"I believe it," Jones said. "Now, why don't you let me walk you to your car? It's late and this isn't the best part of town. In the future, I'll make sure the spot right outside is open for you."

"Okay." Bradley placed her tips into her bag before the two of them walked outside.

Her car was an old, beat-up Toyota. He counted at least three large scratches on just the right side.

"Not that great of a driver?" he asked.

"What?"

He pointed to the scratches.

"Oh, not mine. I got this car super cheap with the scratches, but it's in good shape otherwise. And the inside is clean. It was a starter car for a family's son. Where's your car?"

"I have a car and a motorcycle right out back," he told her.

"Oh, cool. I wanted a bike, but my parents would have died." Bradley laughed. "Do you need a walk to your bike? Need to make sure you make it home safely."

"I live right above the bar."

"Wait, what? You have a very short commute to work then. Bet it saves a lot on gas."

"It does."

The two of them stood there for a moment before Bradley clicked her tongue loudly.

"Well, I should go. It's late. My sister is probably already asleep."

"You live with your sister?"

"No, I'm just staying there until the guy who drugged me is found. They put my name in the papers. It doesn't make me feel as safe."

"Right. Don't blame you. Drive safely, and I'll see you tomorrow evening."

It wasn't until nearly two in the afternoon when Bradley woke up. She realized she hadn't counted her tips from the night before, so she grabbed her purse and pulled the money out. As she counted each bill, she grew more and more amazed. This was more than she ever could have imagined she'd make.

She yawned, still exhausted.

Bradley grabbed her phone and walked to her sister's kitchen to make coffee. Vanessa had one of those fancy coffee pots where you just put in a pod and it made a cup's worth for you. Bradley opened up the drawer with all the pods, overwhelmed with the choices. She finally settled on one and placed it in, setting it up. But nothing came out. She checked the power button and tried again. Still nothing.

She called her sister.

"What's wrong?"

"Why do you assume something is wrong?" Bradley asked.

"You're calling me in the middle of work," Vanessa said.

"Well, I can't get your coffee machine to work."

"Is that all? Bradley, I have a meeting in five minutes I'm preparing for."

"Sorry, I'm just struggling from working until after three. Will you please tell me how to do it?"

Bradley heard typing on the other end of the line. Her sister's voice was muffled for a moment before she returned.

"Did you put water in it?"

"No."

"There ya go. Put water in it, press the button, and it should work. Now, I have to go." Just like that, her sister hung up the phone.

Bradley did as her sister said and the machine began to work. As soon as her cup was full, she poured in some milk and then took a sip.

She walked over to her sister's couch and decided to check her missed messages. She had several from Addison. They were all about the news articles and mentions she'd found of Bradley online.

Even though she knew it was a bad idea, Bradley clicked on the link that led her to a Facebook article. There were over five hundred comments. Every other one was about her and what she'd done wrong, victim-blaming her. She clicked out.

Stop sending me those, Bradley texted her friend. *I don't need to see them.*

Okay. Sorry. How are you?

I'm fine.

And she really was fine. While she worried a little about the man still being out there, she wasn't too affected by what happened. In the end, she hadn't been hurt. But being talked about did bother her. That was the worst part of all of it.

Chapter Five

Vanessa rubbed her eyes with the pads of her fingers. Exhaustion ebbed within her. She checked the time on her computer. She still had another hour until she could sneak out for the day.

Knock. Knock.

Vanessa glanced up, shocked to find Grey standing in her doorway. Her heart skipped a beat and she blinked twice to make sure she wasn't imagining things.

"Grey," she breathed, standing from her chair. "What—"

"Don't stand for me," Grey said with a kind smile. "I was in the building, so I thought I'd stop by to say hello."

He was as gorgeous as ever. His hazel eyes peered back at her, making every bone in her body ache.

"Well, hello," Vanessa said. She searched her brain to find something to say. "Why were you in the building?"

"I had to drop off something for Emma."

"She works in this building?"

"No," Grey said. He sat down on the chair across from her. "She had some paperwork she needed turned in. You know, insurance stuff."

"Oh, right." Her voice came out a bit too high. "So, how long have you known this Emma?"

"A few months. She started working over at the college a little while after we broke up." The words *you broke up with me* lingered in the air, despite being unsaid. Vanessa shifted in her seat.

"Well, that's nice. I'm glad you met."

It fell silent between the two of them. There was so much to say, and yet nothing could be said. Vanessa missed Grey every day, but she knew they could no longer be together. She'd ruined any chance of that.

"And how have you been? I saw your sister's name in the paper. I should have called. Is Bradley okay?"

"Oh! Yes, she's okay," Vanessa said with a nod. "Thankfully, the owner of the bar caught the guy before anything could happen to her and got her to the ER. She's a little frightened of him finding her, so she's staying at my house for a while."

"Are they concerned he could come after her?" Grey asked. He leaned forward, placing his hands on his knees. "Is there anything I can do to help?"

"No," Vanessa said, a bit too quickly. "She's all right. It doesn't seem to be likely that he'll come after her. It just makes her feel safer at my place."

"That's kind of you."

"Just being a big sister." Vanessa let out a shaky breath. "I should get back to work, but it was nice for you to drop by. I've missed you." The words slipped out before she even realized it, and now there was no way for her to take them back. She swallowed hard, touching her lips with her fingers. Grey's eyes met hers intensely as he stood, and she stood with him.

"I've missed you too."

She wanted to go to him—allow him to take her into her arms—but she stopped herself.

"Hopefully, I'll see you again soon."

Grey stood there a beat longer. He then gave her a curt nod and exited her office. Vanessa sunk down into her chair and pressed her hand against her beating chest.

Since she was staying at her sister's, Bradley decided she would make a grocery list of things needed and make dinner for them both later this week. She searched the kitchen for a pen, but couldn't find any. She made her way over to her sister's office. Everything was in its place except the pens. There were none in the pen holder beside her computer.

Bradley opened the skinny top drawer, but it was empty. She sighed. Then she opened the larger drawer. Right on top sat her sister's manuscript. She grinned. Bradley lifted the papers bound with a spiral binding. For months, her sister had worked on this piece of art. It had been Vanessa's pride and joy. Anytime she spoke with her sister, Vanessa would tell her about her progress in her writing. And then she just stopped talking about it. She never mentioned it again after she broke up with Grey.

Now, as she held the manuscript in her hands, she grew curious. Her sister had never told her about the story she was writing, just that she was writing something. She eyed the time.

Her sister wouldn't be home for at least an hour; she could take a small, sneak peek. Bradley sat down on the bench seat by the window and began to read her sister's story.

When Vanessa entered her home, it was quiet. She had guessed her sister would be up by now and getting ready for her evening at work. She went to drop her things off in her office. That's when she found Bradley sitting on her bench seat, reading something. Bradley was so immersed in whatever it was, that she didn't even hear her sister come in.

As Vanessa came closer, she realized exactly what her sister had in her hands.

"What are you doing?" Vanessa growled. She tore the manuscript out of her sister's hands. "Where did you find this?" She could feel her cheeks growing red from anger.

"I was looking for a pen and I found it. It's really good," Bradley said, not even bothered by Vanessa's outburst. "You should publish it."

"It wasn't for you to read! It wasn't for you to look at!" Vanessa yelled.

"But it was just sitting there! Art is meant to be consumed," Bradley argued.

"Not this art," Vanessa disagreed. She walked out of the office and into the kitchen, opening up the trash can.

"Wait!" Bradley called out. "Don't! It's your dream. Don't destroy it."

Vanessa wouldn't hear it. She dropped her manuscript into the trash can, keeping the lid open. She stared at the papers inside the can and felt harsh tears building up behind her eyes. Instead of allowing them to fall, she pushed them back and shook her head.

"It's not my dream. Not anymore," Vanessa said, eerily calm.

"Your dream," Bradley said carefully, "was not silly. Your story is wonderful. You built this beautiful world with beautiful characters—"

"Just stop, please," Vanessa pleaded, finding it harder to keep the tears at bay. "Just leave me alone."

Bradley huffed, but she left Vanessa alone in the kitchen. Vanessa remained in her spot. She couldn't believe her sister went through her things, but even more, she couldn't believe how much she'd overreacted.

She pressed her hands firmly over her face and bent forward. Who was she now? The old Vanessa was calm, collected, and never acted like this.

After giving herself a moment to collect herself, she straightened back up. Since she knew her sister was getting ready for work, Vanessa knew Bradley wouldn't come back. She opened the trash can and pulled her manuscript back out. With her hands, she wiped the trash away and then held it tightly to her chest. She had a backup of her story on her laptop, but this copy was special. It was the one she'd printed out to give to Grey.

She wiped her cheeks her palm before taking the manuscript back to her office. She placed it at the very bottom of her bottom drawer. Then she locked it. While she had no plans of ever doing anything with her story, she was planning on keeping this memento of it forever.

A stray piece of Bradley's hair fell out of its side braid. She tugged down her hair, and then braided it back to one side again. Her white crop top had bundled up on one end, so she adjusted it to allow her two other dragon tattoos to show beneath her chest. The three dragon tattoos she had were a homage to her favorite fictional character. She pulled the waistband of her leggings up and over her belly button ring, not wanting it to catch on anything while she was at work.

Then she checked her hair once more. It would do. Dressing for working at a bar did have its perks. There weren't any rules.

She stepped out of the bedroom, wanting to speak to her sister before leaving. She didn't like that they'd argued. She hadn't meant to upset her.

But when she searched for her sister, she found her locked behind her bedroom door and heard the shower running. She'd have to talk to her tomorrow. Hopefully, the dinner she planned to make her would suffice as an apology.

When she made it to work, she parked where Jones said she should. It was in a lighted spot and right near the front door. It was much safer than where she had parked before. She locked her door and stepped inside the building.

Jones was up on a step stool, adjusting a picture on the wall.

"It's crooked," Bradley said. He glanced down.

"Yeah?"

"Yep. Right side up. Wait, down a bit. There."

Once the picture was adjusted, Jones came down from the stool. It was then that Bradley saw it was a picture of a motor-cycle.

"Is that yours?"

"No. An old customer gave it to me. I thought it would add a little something to this place."

"I guess," Bradley said, glancing around the bar. There wasn't much decoration or theme to it. It just had tables and chairs. The few pictures hanging up didn't really fit together. "Why is this place called Lucky Ones?"

"Not sure. It's what it was named when I bought it. Maybe it has something to do with St. Patrick's Day," he said.

"Hmm, yeah, that would make sense. Savannah does love that holiday."

"Yes, we make it big during that holiday," Jones said.

Bradley chuckled, thinking about the money she'd spent the year before as she'd hung out with her friends. They hadn't even done much, but just the parking alone had been close to a third of her budget for the day.

"Is the clean up afterward worth the money you make?"

"Absolutely."

"Nice, make sure I'm on the calendar for it then."

"Oh, you will be, the entire staff is. We need all hands on deck to survive."

"Yo! You're that girl!" someone called out. Bradley turned around to find a man sitting at the bar with a beer in one hand and his finger pointing at her with the other. "The 'Lucky One.' I saw you in the news!"

Bradley took in a deep breath.

Jones turned toward the customer, his brows furrowed and jaw tight. He started to walk forward, but Bradley placed her hand on his upper arm to stop him.

"He's harmless," Bradley said.

"He needs to mind his own business," Jones disagreed.

This was the first time someone had recognized her in public, but she was sure it wouldn't be the last. She hated that this was how people would look at her now.

"Just let it go," she requested. Jones sighed, but nodded.

"Fine, but I don't like it."

Ever since seeing Grey the other day, thoughts of him consumed Vanessa's mind. They hadn't seen one another in person for months. What made him stop by to see her this particular day? He said it was because he had paperwork to bring to the building, but why then?

She wondered if this was something she was making up in her mind. Perhaps, she was just hoping he'd come by the building just to see her. She remembered the pictures on his social media. It was clear Grey was happy with Emma. Also, he'd mentioned Bradley and what had happened to her. Yes, that was it. He was only checking in on her sister. They had been close, like brother and sister before the break up.

Ring, ring, ring!

She groaned at the sound of her video system ringing. It had been her parents' insistence that she get one so they could call her and see her whenever they wanted. They were the only people she knew who could be calling her.

Reluctantly, she walked over to where the video screen lit up. She'd have to accept the call for them to see or hear her. Part of her wanted to ignore it, but she knew her mother would just call her cell if she didn't answer. Vanessa pulled over a chair, sat down, and answered.

"Oh! There you are!"

Even though they lived only half an hour away, her parents acted like they didn't see her enough. She forced a smile and nodded.

"Yes, I'm here. How are you both?"

"Your dad has been working hard. I've been filling my days with crocheting. Do you think you'll give Grey another chance? I had been hoping for grandbabies soon. It's why I retired."

Vanessa felt her smile falter.

"No, Mom. There's not a future between Grey and me. I'm not having children any time soon."

"You're not getting any younger," her mother said.

"Yes, I know."

This was how it was now since she'd broken up with Grey. Her mother asked her almost every time they saw one another when they would get back together and when she'd have grandbabies. She was unrelenting, not understanding why Vanessa and Grey weren't already back together.

"Do you know what your sister is up to now? She keeps avoiding my phone calls," her mother said. And Vanessa was grateful for the change in topic.

"She has a new job," Vanessa said, trying to keep in mind they weren't supposed to know Bradley was staying with her.

"What type of job?"

"Um, she's working at a bar."

"Ugh." Her mother made a noise before turning around to call out to her father. "She's working at a bar!"

"It's a good gig," Vanessa said, standing up for her sister.

"Well, that's good at least." Her mother wore a sour expression. "I don't know how we'll get her under control. I know you try your best."

"Mom, she's twenty-seven. She's smart. She works hard. Maybe you should give her more credit."

"Vanessa, darling, you really are the best sister." Her mother beamed. "You always look out for her. But truly, she needs to get her life together."

Vanessa inhaled sharply.

"She has," she said.

"If you say so, Vanessa," her mother heavily sighed. "So about Grey…"

Vanessa pretended to hear something behind her. She turned her head and then looked back at her mother.

"Oh, that'll be the plumber. Got to go."

Before giving her mother a chance to respond, she hit the button to end the call.

It was another late, but successful night at Lucky Ones. Bradley counted her tips the moment she parked in front of her sister's house. Tonight she'd made twenty dollars more than the night before. Jones had told her that the money would be even better on weekend nights.

She stepped inside the house and walked over to the couch. As she had been the night before, Vanessa was asleep on it. There was a bowl of ice cream sitting on the table beside the couch. The television was on with an app cued up, yet nothing was playing.

Once again, Bradley turned off the light and put a better blanket over her sister's figure. Then she walked down the hallway and to her sister's bedroom. The bed was made up and looked as though it hadn't been slept in for weeks or even months. While her sister kept a clean house, she'd never been one for making her bed often. Even though she couldn't prove it, she assumed her sister hadn't slept in her own bed for nearly six months now, and that broke her heart.

Chapter Six

B radley spent nearly all day on dinner for her sister. She made one of their childhood favorites: chicken and dumplings. Bradley loved to cook, but she didn't have the space or utilities needed in her apartment for it. Since she had her sister's kitchen at her disposal, she decided she'd cook as a thank you to her sister while also getting the joy of cooking again.

She rolled out the dough for the dumplings, cutting them into little square shapes before dropping them into the large pot. As each dumpling hit the liquid, she gently pushed them down for them to cook. The smell made her mouth water.

The door from the garage opened. Bradley tensed. She hadn't asked if she could use her sister's kitchen and hoped it wouldn't make her angrier at her. Then she reminded herself that it was only her sister. The two of them had fought plenty of times before.

"What's all this? Vanessa asked, entering the kitchen. She placed her hand on her hip and stood taller in her heels, making her nearly a head taller than her. Bradley couldn't read her sister's expression to tell if she was amused or angry.

"I made dinner. Chicken and dumplings. It'll be ready in about half an hour."

"Is this your way of apologizing for going through my things?" Vanessa drew her lips into a thin, unrelenting line.

"Yes?" Bradley said, hopeful it would work.

The line cracked and Vanessa smiled.

"I guess it'll do," she teased. "I overreacted anyway. So I'm sorry." Vanessa's voice was full of sincerity, and Bradley was relieved. Though, really, none of their fights had ever lasted more than a day. They had always been as thick as thieves, unable to stay angry at one another for too long.

"It's all right. And I shouldn't have gone through your things. My curiosity got the best of me. And it still does. Do the fairy and the pirate end up together?" Bradley looked to her sister for an answer.

"Sadly, I can't tell you, Bradley. Some things in life aren't as clear cut as all of that."

Bradley had no idea what her sister meant by that. Was she being cryptic or did her story not have a happy ending?

"I'm going to change, but dinner smells great. I'm starving."

Her sister was back in the kitchen about ten minutes later in her sweatpants and t-shirt, with her hair pulled into a messy bun.

"So how is work with Jones the bar owner?" Vanessa asked. She grabbed a glass and filled it with water from her fridge. "Do you still think he's hot?"

"Well, yes, maybe even more so now. He owns a motorcycle."

Vanessa made a face.

"So, he could die on you at any minute?"

"You're always so positive," Bradley joked. She checked on the dumplings. They were ready.

After she grabbed and filled the bowls, she set them at the kitchen table. Her sister, however, picked hers up.

"Let's just eat in the living room. It's more comfortable there."

"Okay." Bradley grabbed her own bowl and followed her sister to the living room.

They sat down on the couch together, and ate their food in silence at first. Vanessa appeared to be off somewhere in her mind as she took bites of food. Bradley decided to let her be and just eat, while scrolling through her phone.

Per her request, Addison had stopped sending her links to stories about herself. While making dinner, some of her friends had checked in on her again to see how she was doing. She decided not to mention the guy recognizing her in the bar to them or Vanessa. It would just make them worry.

"I saw Grey yesterday," Vanessa said a moment later. Bradley jerked her eyes up to look at her sister, surprised she hadn't mentioned it before now.

"What? When? Where?"

"At my work," Vanessa answered, knitting her brows. "That's strange, isn't it? He said he was there to drop off some paper work for Emma."

"And Emma is the new girlfriend?"

"Yes."

"Oh." Bradley pondered this. "Did he say anything else?" She watched her sister thoughtfully.

"Not really." Vanessa spun her spoon in her bowl a few times before setting it down on the table in front of her. She took in a deep breath before whispering, "I told him I missed him. Why would I say that?"

"Because you do?"

"Well, of course, I do. We dated for three years. We talked about marriage and having a family, but—" Vanessa shook her head. She sunk back, deep into the cushions. Her eyes moved to a corner in the room and her lower lip began to quiver.

Bradley set down her bowl, moving closer to her sister.

"I'm sorry," Vanessa murmured. "I've been fine, truly I have. But I just don't know what's gotten into me lately."

"Do you think what happened to me could have triggered something?" Bradley cautiously asked.

"No," her sister said, though the lack of convention made Bradley believe otherwise. She pulled her sister into her arms, right before Vanessa let out a loud sob.

"Why was I such an idiot?"

Bradley wanted to reply that she wasn't. However, she knew it wouldn't matter what she said at this moment. Her sister wouldn't hear what she had to say. Instead, she just held her and allowed her to cry.

Vanessa hated the loud sound of her alarm going off in the mornings, especially after a restless sleep. She turned around on the couch and grabbed her phone, hitting the button to turn off the sound.

Her blanket was warm, making her not want to get out of the couch. She closed her eyes momentarily and enjoyed feeling warm and content. It was only then she recalled crying in her sister's arms the night before. A flush of embarrassment covered her. It had been six months. It was time to move on.

She stood up, folding the blanket and placing it back on its spot on the back of the couch. She raised her hands with a yawn, surprised when she spotted her sister standing at the end of the hallway with her phone in her hands.

"Why are you up this early?"

"The police station called. They want me to come in. They think they found the guy who drugged me," Bradley said. She held a puzzled expression on her face and kept messing with the stud earring in her ear.

"Oh," Vanessa replied, sensing her sister's apprehension. "I can come with you."

"Are you sure? You already missed work on Saturday." Bradley's hand dropped from her ear. She gave a grateful smile.

"It's fine." Vanessa shrugged it off. "I have a lot of time off I haven't used. I'll just call in sick." Her job, while grueling at times, was understanding. Every other Saturday was a work day, but in return, they got more flexibility when it came to working in the middle of the week. She was fortunate to have found such a job.

"Okay, I really would like you to come with me."

Her normally unbothered sister looked pale. Vanessa walked up to her and placed her hand on her shoulder, giving it a supportive squeeze.

"And I will. I'll be right by your side."

She didn't expect to be this nervous. She'd only met the man briefly at the bar before Jones stepped in and saved the day. This all should be easy; just identify him and go back to her sister's place. But it wasn't easy. Her body felt like jelly. She was about to face the man who drugged her drink, who wanted to hurt her—*assault* her. Her stomach flipped.

Her hand rested on the door handle, but she couldn't find it in her to open the door. Her breathing grew harsher. Why was this so terrifying?

"We don't have to rush," Vanessa said, taking her hand in hers. "We can sit here until you're ready."

Her sister's words gave her the push she needed.

"I think it's better if I just get it over with," Bradley told Vanessa before pulling her hand away from hers. She opened the door and stepped out of the car. It was bright outside, making her squint her eyes. Her sister walked over to her and took her hand again.

"I'm following your lead," Vanessa assured her.

Bradley was more than grateful for her sister's support in this matter. She wasn't sure she'd have been able to do this all on her own. Her hand squeezed tighter around Vanessa's as they got closer to the door.

After they entered the building, Bradley told them who she was and why she was there. They told her to take a seat and they would call her back in a moment. The moment she sat down, her knees started to bounce.

"After this, we could grab a bite to eat. We could go to Marshalls. I know you love their waffles," Vanessa said. She gave Bradley a supportive grin.

"Sure." But Bradley didn't feel hungry. Her eyes glanced up at the clock. With every tick, her stomach constricted.

Finally, about ten minutes later, they were called back. She was led to a room that reminded her of movie and television scenes, where someone stands behind one sided glass to pick out which number the criminal is behind. It felt surreal—like she couldn't be the one standing here and identifying the perpetrator.

She inched forward slowly, though she knew they couldn't see her. There were five men, all standing in a row with a number in each of their hands. Her breath hitched. He was right there. He wasn't looking forward, but instead, moving his head around from side to side, acting as nonchalant as possible.

Her heart began to race. There stood the man who drugged her; the man who stripped her own bodily autonomy from her by slipping something into her drink. Her throat grew dry and she had to breathe deeply to keep her composure.

"Number 2," she said, breathless. "That's him."

"Are you sure, Ms. Price?"

"Absolutely sure," she answered. "I'd remember that face anywhere."

His eyes moved to where she stood. She swallowed hard and backed up, feeling her sister place her hand on her lower back.

"Thank you."

"Is there anything else you need from me?" she asked.

"Not right now. You're free to go."

Vanessa was glad that was over. Even though it hadn't been about her, she'd felt uneasy the entire time they were in the station. Her mind kept traveling to a place she didn't want it to go. In order to try and keep it under control, she'd focused on helping her sister through it. Poor Bradley had been pale through the whole thing, but once they stepped outside, she seemed more at ease.

The breakfast place was just a few blocks over, so they decided to walk. It was a nice day, and they both could use the time to clear their heads. When they entered the restaurant, Vanessa spotted Bradley's new boss right away. He sat alone at a booth, eating a large plate full of waffles. He wore a polo shirt, which Vanessa never would have imagined he'd wear. She pictured him only in tight, white t-shirts and leather jackets.

Bradley lit up, so Vanessa obliged her and walked with her over to his table. He saw them and gave them a warm smile.

"I didn't expect to see you here," Jones said.

"Had to go to the police station to identify the guy who drugged me," Bradley told him.

"And was it him?"

"It was," Bradley said.

"I just got my own call from the station. Looks like they want me to also pick him out of the line-up."

"Oh?" Bradley asked.

"Makes sense, I guess. You were drugged, Bradley. Jones was the only one who was completely sober," Vanessa said.

"Why don't you guys sit with me?" Jones offered. "It's pretty busy. This will get you fed faster."

"Are you sure you don't mind?" Vanessa asked. She pulled on the edge of her top. Unlike her sister, Vanessa felt uncomfortable around people she hardly knew.

"Please, sit."

She and Bradley slid onto the bench seat across from Jones.

"Do you come here often?" Bradley asked. "It's one of our favorite places to eat."

"No, I just discovered it recently."

"Great discovery, isn't it?"

Vanessa glanced between her sister and Jones, not knowing what to say or add to the conversation. Her fingers anxiously tugged on one another in her lap.

"Did you grow up here in Savannah?" Bradley asked Jones.

"No," he answered. "I lived up in North Carolina. I came down here a few years ago when there was an offer for this bar at a good price."

"Have you always owned a bar?" Vanessa surprised herself by asking a question.

"No, but it was always a dream of mine. I like the hours. And I like the area down here. I'd always wanted to move to Savannah. Two birds, one stone."

The waiter came by and took their orders. They always ordered the same thing. Bradley got waffles with a side of sausage, and Vanessa got the breakfast mini meal which consisted of eggs, one small pancake, and some bacon.

"Does your family live in North Carolina? And what part of North Carolina?" Bradley asked after they ordered.

"Near Wilmington, and yes. My father and brother still live up that way. My mom passed when I was ten." Jones paused for a moment. His fingers rubbed along his beard. Vanessa watched as Jones's face softened at the memory of his mother.

"That must have been hard," Bradley said.

"It was. Still miss her, but my dad, brother, and I are close."

"That's good. Maybe I should move hours away from my parents. Then they might like me more," Bradley teased. Vanessa gently nudged her with her shoulder.

"They love you."

"They may love me, but they do not like me."

When their food came, Vanessa's stomach growled. She took a bite of the eggs and happily sighed. There wasn't much better than the eggs from Marshalls.

Jones finished up his meal soon after they got theirs. He stood from the table, excusing himself, saying he would be right back.

"You have a crush," Vanessa sung, playfully.

"Maybe," Bradley said, raising her eyebrows. "But I'll have to leave it at that. He is my boss."

"Of a company he owns. Pretty sure you don't have to worry about HR in this situation."

Before they could say anything else, Jones came back. He stood at the edge of the booth, placing his right hand on the table and leaning over slightly.

"Thanks for the conversation. The meal has been paid."

"You didn't have to do that," Vanessa said.

"I wanted to," Jones answered with a kind smile. "See you tonight, Bradley. And Vanessa, feel free to swing by anytime for a free drink."

He gave them a wink before walking away.

"He is nice," Vanessa said. "Plus he did that whole, saving your life thing."

"He did." Bradley lifted her drink, taking a sip. "And he's handsome. I love him in his little polo shirt with the tattoos down his arms."

"Maybe you two will get matching tattoos."

"Oh! Maybe."

They both laughed. Vanessa was glad the day had turned around into a happier one for her sister.

CHAPTER SEVEN

Now that her attacker had been arrested, Bradley felt safe to go back to her apartment. She knew the guy would likely make bail until his trial, but she wasn't as concerned about him coming after her. If anything happened to her, they'd know it was him.

But she did feel lonely. Even though they'd only spent a few hours a day together, it had been nice being with her sister more. They'd spent every evening together, talking and gossiping about everything and nothing at all.

Also, since being at her sister's place, she found her worry for her sister had grown. Being with her made it easier to see how withdrawn from the world she'd become since the incident back in the fall.

With a sigh, Bradley placed her bag back onto her bed. She needed to take a nap to be ready for work tonight, but her mind remained on her sister. Perhaps she should have stayed one extra night.

A moment later her phone rang.

"Miss me already?" Bradley asked her sister.

"I do," she said. "Are you sure you feel safe enough?"

"Yes. But you can come and stay the night with me if it'll make you feel better."

"As long as you're okay with being on your own, I'll leave you be."

"You know," Bradley began, "since I'm no longer there, you could sleep in the guest bedroom instead of on the couch."

Her sister didn't respond.

"I wish you'd talk to someone," Bradley pressed on. "I only worry about you because I love you."

"There's nothing to worry about." Her sister's voice was strained. "I just have to come to terms with the damage I caused. And I am. I'm doing better."

"Right," Bradley said, knowing nothing she said would work. "Are you lonely at your house all alone? I could come over or you could stay with me."

"No, I'm fine. Goodnight, Bradley."

Bradley frowned. She should have insisted her sister come and stay with her. Perhaps being together, Bradley could have gradually helped her sister come to terms with what really happened.

Jones rarely gave himself time off work. His business stayed open every day of the week. Even though they didn't stay open on Sunday nights, they were open for business at lunchtime. It was hard work, but he didn't mind it. Work was all he knew. He'd been working since he was old enough to help his dad put food on the table.

His workers became his family. And so to him, he had all he needed with his job.

"What do you do for fun?" Bradley asked. Jones looked up, twisting his lips.

"Fun?"

"Yes, like what are your hobbies? I like to paint. I've been working on this huge mural in my apartment. I'm not technically supposed to paint in there, but my landlord let it slide because I'm a decent painter."

"I have this bar and my bike," Jones answered. "I also like to read."

"Oh? What types of books?" Bradley pestered.

"Does it matter?" Jones asked. Books had always been one of his favorite things. As a young boy, he could remember going to the library with his mother and spending hours looking through all the different sections. Even after her death, he kept going. Now, his walls were filled with books from top to bottom, overflowing the shelves.

"Well, when do you read?"

"After shifts, mornings, whenever I get a chance," Jones told her, scowling. How did she always get him to reveal more about himself?

"So you really, *really* like reading. Why don't I ever see you with a book?" Bradley asked curiously.

"Don't want anything to spill on it," Jones answered honestly.

"Do you like to go and visit your family?"

"Sometimes. I don't have much time though, because of the job."

"No one here could cover for you? Like Mads? I know you trust him."

"You're really chatty, aren't you?"

Bradley shrugged. Today she wore one of her spaghetti strap tops that showed off the larger dragon tattoo on her shoulder. He knew better than to ask her about it, or else she'd go on a tirade about how her favorite character on some television show was done dirty.

"And you're very quiet," she said back at him. She took the dried cup from his hand and placed it on the shelf.

"Not much to say," he answered.

"Surely, you have something to say," Bradley said, wiggling her eyebrows.

"What would I say? You know everything you can about me."

"I don't even know your name," Bradley countered.

"You don't need to know that. You know what you need to know," Jones said, leaving it at that.

Thankfully, they lapsed into a silence.

Lucky Ones didn't open for another half-hour. With Bradley added to their staff, they were able to do their opening smoother than before they had her. It no longer felt like a rush to get everything done last minute. Now, the last half-hour was usually quiet and calm.

"Is your sister all right?" he randomly asked, not quite knowing where the question came from. He hardly knew Vanessa, yet he found himself thinking about her often. There was something about the way she always seemed like a scared animal whenever he saw her.

Bradley paused what she was doing. She was turned away from him stacking up the cups. She took a deep breath before dropping her hand and turning to face him.

"No," she answered honestly. "She's not." Her face grew solemn. "She's not at all."

"Did something happen?" Jones cursed himself internally. It wasn't in his nature to ask questions about other people.

"Yes," Bradley said. "But I can't tell you about it. She's only told me, so I'm the only one who's allowed to know."

"That must be difficult," Jones sympathized.

"It is," Bradley replied, tucking a strand of hair behind her ear. "I love her, very much, you know? She's stubborn and has a lot of issues. Know how I said my parents don't really like me?"

Jones nodded.

"It's because I'm the *disappointment*," she said, using air quotes. "But it's the opposite for Vanessa. She's their perfect child. They expect her to be perfect in every way. It has put so much pressure on her that she experienced something traumatic and she refuses to face it. I worry about her, about what this will do to her. She's already not herself. Heck, you even noticed and you hardly know her."

"I can tell you love her."

"I do."

"It's good the way your parents see you hasn't caused a rift between the two of you. It easily could, being treated so differently."

"I guess." Bradley shrugged. "But she's always been good to me. Never treated me as different. She even held my hand when I got my first tattoo."

"The dragon?"

Bradley laughed.

"No, the stars. She's a good big sister. It's time I take care of her."

Jones nodded. He thought about his brother and dad in North Carolina. Even though he didn't see them as often as he'd like, he did try to take care of them in the ways he could, sending some of the money the bar made to them. Sometimes he wondered if he wasn't doing enough.

Bradley stepped into her apartment when the sun was already starting to rise. Friday nights at Lucky Ones were exhausting. She kicked off her shoes and then fell right into her bed. With her pillow, she covered her face to hide from the sun coming through her blinds.

In an instant, she was asleep.

Only three hours later, was she awoken by the sounds of her phone ringing. She hit at it, trying to get it to stop making such a high pitched noise in her ear. But it didn't work. Instead, her hand hit it, causing it to fly off her bedside table and against the wall. Somehow, it made the sound louder.

She tightened her pillow over her head. Eventually, it would have to go to voicemail. It rang two more times before stopping. She readjusted herself on the bed and tried to go back to sleep. However, before she could get comfortable, her phone began ringing again.

With a huff, Bradley sat herself up and stumbled out of the bed. Her eyes struggled to adjust to the brightness in the room.

She finally grabbed the phone and answered it without checking to see who had called her.

"Hello?" she angrily asked.

"Bradley, dear, you aren't still asleep are you? It's nearly 8."

She wanted to scream.

"I didn't get home until 5 in the morning, so yes, I was still sleeping when you called," Bradley told her mother. She pressed her thumb on the spot in between her eyebrows to try and relieve some of the building pressure of her oncoming headache.

"You really should get a job that gets you home at a decent time, Bradley. How are you supposed to settle down working such odd hours?"

"I don't know, Mom," she said with a roll of her eyes. "Do you need something?"

"No, it's just that tomorrow your sister and I are going to brunch. I thought you could join us."

"Sorry, I can't. I have…." Bradley tried to come up with a good excuse. She would be working another late night. She knew the last thing she'd want in the morning was to spend time with her mother telling her what all she needed to change to become the person she expected her to be. "I'm working late again." She decided to tell the truth. "I'll still be asleep when you guys go to brunch. Sorry."

"Oh," her mother said. "Well, maybe another time. Love you, dear. Get some rest."

"Love you too." Bradley hung up her phone and made sure it was set to silent.

Then she went back to sleep.

CHAPTER EIGHT

Sunday brunches with mother were always an event. They were scheduled once a month and had been going on for nearly five years now. They went to the same location every time—a local café—and her mother expected them to be dressed up and to pay for her.

Sometimes Bradley came along, but most times she found an excuse to miss it. Vanessa never had that luxury. She missed one time, six months ago, and her mother never let her live it down.

Today for brunch, Vanessa chose a long, flowery, summer dress and small sweater. Then she drew her hair up into a nice, low bun, leaving a few hairs loose to frame her face. She even added some lipstick so her mother wouldn't make a comment about the lack of color on her face.

She sat in the parking lot for fifteen minutes. She always arrived early, but never exited her car until she saw her mother's car pull into the parking lot. She checked the time and glanced around the parking lot again. Finally, she spotted her mother's car.

With a heavy breath, Vanessa got out of her car. She forced herself to smile and she waved. Her mother pulled in to the parking spot over in the corner. Then she got out and walked over to Vanessa, wearing one of her many dress suits. This one was cream colored, with small pink and blue flowers along the skirt.

"I called your sister yesterday to join us, but she's working too late. Honestly, Vanessa, can you believe she has such a job?"

"Come on, Mom," Vanessa said, holding back a sigh.

The moment they stepped inside, they were taken back to the same booth where they always sat.

"It's a bit drafty in here," her mother complained.

"We can change seats," Vanessa said, pretending like her mother didn't say that every time.

"Oh no, dear." Her mother shook her head. "This is where I can see everything. I'll survive."

Vanessa glanced over the menu. It hadn't changed in the last five years, but it gave her somewhere to focus her attention.

"Have you been sleeping?" her mother asked. "You have bags under your eyes and you look terrible."

"Well, thanks Mom." Vanessa rolled her eyes.

"I didn't mean it like that. I just worry about you. You were supposed to marry Grey, but instead you broke up with him. You've lost too much weight. That dress is almost falling off of you. And now you look like you're not sleeping."

"I'm fine," Vanessa bit. "I already told you, Grey and I were not a good fit. And the rest is just....I'm fine." She shook her head. *I'm fine* seemed to be her mantra lately. But she *was* fine.

She was tired of people insisting she was not. "What are you going to order? Your regular?"

The change of topic seemed to work, because her mother returned her attention to the menu in her hands. Vanessa knew exactly what she would order; she never went off script. Her mother was always predicable.

"I think I'll get the club sandwich with tomato soup and a mimosa. It is brunch, isn't it?" she asked playfully, as if she was being mischievous for ordering alcohol at 10:30 in the morning.

"Sounds good. I think I'm just going to do the eggs and toast today with an apple juice."

"No mimosa? You used to always enjoy getting those with me," her mother said with a little pout.

"Nope. I've told you many times, I decided to stop drinking."

"One mimosa is not drinking."

Vanessa sucked in a deep breath. They went over this every time.

"Will you please just let it go? I don't want to have a drink."

"Alright, alright. Don't get yourself in a hissy. That's your sister's sort of thing."

"Why do you do that?" Vanessa asked, angrily. "Why must you always take shots at Bradley? She's not even here, and you've found a way to talk badly about her."

Her mother sat back, not used to Vanessa speaking so abruptly.

"Bradley is a good daughter and a good sister. She works hard. She doesn't do drugs. She treats people with kindness. I don't understand why you don't see it," Vanessa continued. Her body shook from the adrenaline and anxiousness of speaking out of turn, but she also felt a sense of pride in herself for saying what she wanted to say. Her lips quirked up.

"I do see those things, Vanessa. See, this is what I'm talking about. Something isn't right with you. Has someone done something? Was it Grey?"

Vanessa hit her hands on the table, making their water glasses shake.

"No. No one has done anything. I'm just tired of you talking about my sister like that. She's your daughter. Be kinder to her."

The waitress came up to the table to take their orders, ending their harsh conversation. Vanessa no longer felt hungry, but she knew she couldn't just storm off. She waited for her mother to give her order before giving her own.

"I do love Bradley," her mother said after the waitress left. "She's my baby girl. And I love you. I do wish you'd tell me what is going on with you." Her mother tapped her fingers on top of the table before sliding them over to rest on top of Vanessa's hand. "You haven't been the same since you ended it with Grey. You even missed our brunch date that week."

"Yes, I know, Mom." Vanessa forced a smile. "I remember. Things just changed, but I am fine. I'm very happy. Content," she amended.

"Well, as long as you're sure." Her mother eyed her curiously. Vanessa knew she was looking for something else to say about it.

"I am."

"Good, but if…" her mother paused. She shook her head and gave Vanessa a grin. "Well, now, we can just enjoy our brunch, can't we?"

"Sure."

Since her sister was drugged a week ago, Vanessa found it hard to get a full night's sleep. She woke up several times throughout the night, panicked, as if she'd had a nightmare. Her heart would be racing and her forehead sweating, but the nightmare was always gone the moment she opened her eyes. It slipped from her memories, almost as though it was trying to protect her from herself.

Tonight when she awoke, her television was still on and playing a show on streaming, which meant it hadn't been long since she'd fallen asleep. Vanessa turned off the television. Then she sat in silence.

Her house was so quiet now. Loneliness seeped in. She always felt lonely.

It was after ten. For a moment, she debated calling Bradley, but then she decided against it. Her sister would only bring up the fact Vanessa couldn't sleep. Vanessa didn't need that hard look in the mirror.

Are you up? she texted Grey before she could stop herself. It was too late to take it back, so now she stared at her phone in nervous anticipation of him responding to her. Part of her hoped he was asleep and in the morning he would ignore her late night text. However, another, larger part of her, hoped he would reply right now.

A few minutes later and with no response, Vanessa sat her phone down, letting out a relieved breath of air. This was for the best. She stood, stretching, and decided to make herself some warm tea. Sometimes that could help her get back to sleep on a particularly difficult night.

The moment she turned on the stove, her phone dinged. Her heart fell. She raced to her phone and picked it up.

I am. Is everything alright?

Vanessa chewed on the inside of her lip. What she said now could change everything. Carefully, she lifted her phone.

Yes. Sorry, I texted so late. I couldn't sleep and I didn't know who else to message.

It's fine. Do you need to talk?

This was her moment. They could talk. Everything would be better, Grey and she could get back together, and Emma would be nothing but a mere memory. But as she started to text that yes, she needed to talk, she decided against it. What would they talk about? Certainly not the truth, and isn't that why she broke up with him? She wouldn't tell him—*couldn't* tell him.

No. I'm sorry I bothered you. Goodnight, Grey.

Are you sure?

Yes. Goodnight.

Alright, goodnight, Ness. Sleep well.

Vanessa read over the messages a few times. She then sat her phone back on the table before heading back into the kitchen to make her tea.

When Vanessa woke up the next morning, there was another message from Grey. She saw his name on her screen and swiped right so his message would pop up. Her breath hitched in anticipation for what it would say.

I'm always here, Ness. I'll always be here.

Her hand covered her mouth. There were so many things she needed to say and needed to tell him. But as she thought about what to say to him, another text popped up.

You're my friend. I'm here for you.

Friend. The single word hurt her heart. She should be grateful he even wanted to be friends with her after she broke up with him without any warning.

I know, she responded. *But I'm fine. Thanks for being my friend.* She put her phone on the coffee table and stood up.

Since she had a while before needing to be at work, Vanessa turned on the television. Her sister's face filled the screen.

"What the..," she said to herself, sitting back down and turning up the volume.

They call her the 'Lucky One.' Bradley Price was the woman who escaped the serial rapist, Allen Carter. While at the bar Lucky Ones, the owner of the bar, Jones, caught Carter trying to leave with a drugged Price. She is the only girl to have escaped this rapist's grasp.

Vanessa turned off the television. It felt unreal, seeing her sister's picture like that and being spoken about in such a way. While it was a miracle her sister had been saved, it still didn't seem like anyone should know her business. Vanessa knew if it had been her, she wouldn't want anyone to know.

A nagging voice started speaking in the back of her mind, but she shoved it away. She hated that nagging voice trying to make her feel things she didn't want to face; things she refused to believe. She knew it came from her sister insisting things that she didn't understand.

Vanessa shook her head. At moments like these, she missed having a glass of wine. It would have helped take the nagging voice away.

CHAPTER NINE

It had now been five weeks since she'd started her job at Lucky Ones. Tonight was her first weekend night off. To celebrate, she was going out with her friends to any place but the one where she worked.

Tomorrow night her friend, Addison, was getting married, giving Bradley two nights off in a row. She knew she should probably rest tonight since tomorrow was a big day, but her friend wanted one last hurrah before her wedding.

Addison picked Bradley up from her place. It was nice to have an evening with friends; an evening where she didn't have any worries in the world. She hoped she didn't have any more run-ins with people recognizing her. Since the time in the bar, there had been a couple more. Though, they were all less obnoxious than the first, whispering to the person with them and glancing at her. None of the others had come up to her.

They went to a nice restaurant downtown to begin their fun. With Bradley being drugged, the group decided to institute a few rules to keep everyone safe. The first was a buddy system. The buddy was not to leave their side, unless they were with another safe friend. Also, all drinks had to be picked up by them and taken to their seats, unless brought by someone who worked there.

"I hate that it's like this," Addison said as they stepped out of their car. "The world really isn't safe for us girls, is it?"

Bradley grimaced.

"I guess it's not."

They went inside to find the rest of their party already seated. Bradley was determined to not let what happened ruin her evening. Her life wouldn't be controlled by one instance, caused by one, pathetic man.

Their table was long and in the middle of the restaurant. One of their friends had tied gold and silver balloons to each chair, making sure to draw even more attention to them. Bradley sat down, ready to have fun. They paid in advance for their food, so she knew all she had to pay for tonight were drinks.

She happened to look up and spot Grey across the room, sitting with Emma. Her curiosity got the better of her and she couldn't look away. The two sat across from one another in a corner booth, both grinning. Grey's hand reached across the table, bringing it up to gently touch Emma's cheek. She blushed before taking his hand and kissing his knuckles.

"Do you think they look happy?" Bradley turned to her friend Addison, who sat beside her. Addison glanced up from the menu of items they'd been given to choose from and followed where Bradley was pointing. She narrowed her eyes, trying to get a look at a couple.

"Yes," Addison said assuredly. "Why? Do we know them?"

"Addison, that's Grey."

Addison's eyes narrowed even more.

"Oh! Oooooh!" she screeched. "Vanessa's Grey?"

Bradley shushed her. The last thing they needed was for Grey to spot them and realize they were talking about him. Addison gave her a sheepish look.

"Sorry. Is Vanessa all torn up about him dating her?"

"Yes."

"But she broke up with him, right?"

"Yes."

"Bummer. I was rooting for them. But yes, they look happy. I mean, look at how they are looking at one another. If I didn't know any better, I'd say they were a newly married couple. They have that early love glow about them."

"Yeah," Bradley sighed. They really did.

When they stepped outside after dinner, Bradley saw Grey standing alone by the corner, rocking on his heels.

"Hey," she whispered to Addison, "I'll meet you at the bar."

"But we're supposed to have eyes on one another at all times."

"I know, I know. I'll be with Grey. He's right there. The bar is literally right across the street and it isn't even late yet. I'll be there in ten minutes or less."

"You better or I'm coming after you."

"Deal," Bradley said before walking over to where Grey stood. He noticed her immediately and smiled.

"I saw you at dinner," he said, "but I didn't want to bother you while you were with your friends. How have you been?" Grey had always been kind to Bradley. In many ways, he'd been like a big brother to her. When he and Vanessa broke up, she felt a deep sadness over never spending time with him again.

"Fine," she answered. "I'm sure you've seen the news."

"I have. I should have checked on you. I'm sorry—" He reached out, pausing halfway before dropping his arm to his side.

"Don't apologize. I know things became awkward after you and Vanessa broke up. I don't expect to hear from you all the time or anything."

"Well, I am sorry for what happened. Are you alright?" His words were sincere.

"I am."

"What about Ness? She messaged me a few weeks back, later in the evening. It was strange," he said.

"Yeah?" This was news to her. "What did she say?"

Grey licked his lower lip and let out a low breath.

"I...she just seemed out of sorts, is all," he said. Bradley nodded.

"I think what happened to me caused her to—" She stopped herself.

"Caused her to what?" Grey took a small step forward, his face full of concern and curiosity. Bradley swallowed hard.

"I don't know," Bradley lied. "Doesn't matter." She decided she needed to change the subject. If Grey asked more questions, she might break and tell him the truth. "You look happy. Your new girlfriend is pretty."

"Thank you. I am."

"Good. That's really good, Grey. I'm glad you're happy. But do you miss her?" Bradley couldn't believe those words came out of her mouth. What had happened to changing the subject from her sister?

"Of course I miss her, Bradley," he answered, sticking his hands deep into his pockets. "But she left me. I planned on spending my life with her, and she just up and ended it. I'm allowed to find happiness elsewhere."

Bradley inhaled sharply, surprised at how hurt he sounded.

"I know," she whispered. "I wish things had been different."

"Me too."

"Well, hello," a female voice sounded from behind Bradley. Emma walked around her and hooked her arm around Grey's. She rested her head on Grey's upper arm, smiling at Bradley. "I don't think we've met."

"Emma," Grey began, "this is Bradley, Vanessa's little sister. Bradley, this is Emma."

Emma straightened up and brought her hand out for Bradley to shake.

"Oh! I've heard so much about you. Love your dragon tattoo! My brother is a tattoo artist, let me know if you are getting a new one and I can get you a discount." Emma's bubbly and kind personality was not what Bradley expected.

"Thanks, I will," Bradley said. "What do you do?"

"I work at the college, but not in sciences like Grey. I'm not quite that smart. I work in admissions. We met in the cafeteria a few months ago." Again, her arm went around Grey's, holding him close. But it wasn't in a protective, *don't come near my man* way. It was more in a, *I can't get enough of him* type of way.

"Cool." While Bradley probably could speak with Emma for a while longer, it felt like she was betraying her sister if she did. "Well, I should probably go. My friends are waiting for me at the bar. But it was nice to meet you, and Grey, nice to see you again."

"Of course! Maybe we could do lunch some time," Emma said. "And invite your sister."

"Maybe. Good evening."

Even though she'd been out late, Bradley decided to swing by her sister's place the next morning. She stopped and grabbed doughnuts from the local bakery before knocking on her door.

When the door opened, Bradley's eyes widened in shock. Vanessa looked sickly. Her cheeks were sunk in and there were dark rings around her eyes. She wore a pink, fluffy robe around herself.

"You look like shit? Are you sick?"

"No," Vanessa answered. She moved out of the way for Bradley to come inside.

As Bradley entered, her eyesight had to adjust. It was dark. All of the shades in her sister's house were drawn and the only light came from the television, which was playing reruns of an older show. On the coffee table were sleep aids and several used tissues. The house was very different than how it used to be. Her sister usually kept it bright and airy, always ready for guests.

"I know we haven't seen each other much over the past month, but this isn't normal," Bradley said. "Why have you been avoiding me, anyway?"

"I haven't," Vanessa said, furrowing her brows. "I've been busy with work."

"Uh huh."

Bradley walked over to the large window in Vanessa's living room and ripped open the curtains.

"Sit." It was said as more of a command than an invitation. Her sister didn't say a word, just slipped down and onto the couch, pulling a blanket over her lap.

"Thanks for bringing breakfast." Vanessa took a doughnut from the box and took a large bite. "These are always the best ones."

"They are." Bradley eyed her sister carefully. "Have you not been sleeping?"

"Not really," Vanessa said. She rubbed the back of her neck with the back of her hand. "I've just been really focused on this thing at work."

Bradley watched her sister, noting how over the past several weeks, she'd been slowly becoming more and more unraveled.

"You're a terrible liar," Bradley told her.

"What is today?"

"Changing the subject are we?"

Vanessa stood, her hands coming together in front of her as she began to panic.

"I'm late. Mom is going to kill me."

Bradley stood up beside her sister.

"Wait, calm down. What do you mean?"

"Brunch."

"Don't you do brunch on Sundays after church?" Bradley asked.

"Yes."

"It's Saturday."

"Oh."

"Sit back down."

Her sister did as she was told, sitting on the edge of her seat. She gnawed on the side of her thumb. Bradley noticed how raw the skin around all her fingers were. She moved closer to her and pulled her hand away from her mouth.

"I'm fine," Vanessa said in a rebuttal. Bradley let out a low laugh.

"Fine? Sure. All of this is totally normal behavior."

"As I said, I'm just stressed about work. And I need sleep. I can't sleep because all I think about is…work."

Bradley sat down next to her sister, drawing her hand into her lap.

"Do you want to talk about it?"

Her sister shook her head.

"Okay." Bradley pulled her sister closer so her head rested on her lap. Bradley ran her fingers through her sister's tangled hair. "I'll do brunch with mom tomorrow."

"What?"

"Yes. I'll call her when I leave here, tell her you are sick, but that I'll go. That will keep her off your back for the month, won't it?"

"Are you sure you want to do that?"

"I don't want to do it, no, but I will. Maybe without that worry over your head, you can sleep better tonight."

"Maybe."

Bradley continued to run her fingers through her sister's hair. She could feel her sister relaxing beneath her. Perhaps she should have come by more often. She had been trying to give Vanessa space, but what she needed was someone checking in on her.

"I saw Grey last night."

Vanessa tensed beneath her.

"Oh?"

"And Emma. What a bitch," Bradley said with a shake of her head. "Like, total bitch, annoying, rude person."

Vanessa turned so her back was on the couch and she could look up at Bradley.

"Really? She's that awful?"

"I mean, no, but she's not you."

"So you're being the protective sister?" Vanessa smiled slightly before it faltered. "Grey really is happy with her, isn't he? And she's a great person, isn't she?"

"Yeah," Bradley regretfully said. Vanessa turned back to her side.

"What a bitch," she said beneath her breath. Bradley laughed, both out of shock from hearing her sister curse and just because there was some lightness to her words. "I do want him to be happy."

"I know you do," Bradley said.

"I love him, but I hurt him. And it's too late to make it right, now." Vanessa let out a shaky breath.

"I bet if you sat him down and explained everything to him, he would be more understanding than you think he will."

Bradley felt a tear land on her leg. Her sister didn't respond. Bradley continued to run her fingers through Vanessa's hair as she watched the old sitcom on the television. Over time, her sister's tears subsided when she fell into a restless sleep. Not wanting to wake her, Bradley carefully replaced her legs with a pillow and placed a blanket over her sister's figure.

As quietly as possible, she snuck out of the house, making a note to check in on her sister more often.

Chapter Ten

Vanessa woke up feeling more refreshed than she had in weeks. She rubbed beneath her eyelids and tried to remember what day it was. There on her coffee table sat the doughnuts her sister brought her earlier—or was it yesterday? It all blurred together.

She grabbed her phone. It was still Saturday, but now three in the afternoon. She'd slept around five hours.

Ring! Ring!

"Great," she said beneath her breath. She walked over to the tablet and pressed the button to accept her mother's call.

"Oh, you *do* look bad. Should I bring you over some soup? Bradley called me, said you were sick."

"No. Don't come by. I don't want to get you sick," she said almost too quickly, earning a suspicious glare from her mother. "I just need some rest and then I'll be better."

"Are you sure? I don't like the idea of you all alone in that house," her mother said, frowning.

"Mom, I'm fine," Vanessa told her. "I'm already feeling much better, Bradley took care of me this morning."

"I know, what a good sister she is."

Vanessa lifted her brow. She couldn't recall the last time her mother gave her sister a compliment. It was nice to hear.

"She is," Vanessa agreed. "She brought me breakfast and made sure I got some rest. Sadly, I won't be able to make it to brunch tomorrow."

"Oh, I know. Bradley told me. She's going to come instead. It'll be nice to see her. Did you know I haven't seen her in person since she was in the hospital?"

"I did not." Vanessa yawned. She could go back to sleep and probably sleep all night if she laid down right now.

"You're still tired. Get some rest, dear. I'll call you tomorrow to check on you. Love you."

"Love you too."

Vanessa made a note to thank her sister for taking over brunch and bringing her breakfast.

Even though she wanted to sleep more, she decided she should put her house back in order before that. Over the past several weeks, she'd let things slide. She hadn't done the dishes right away, and she was behind on laundry. She couldn't live like this. It seemed like ever since Bradley was drugged, she couldn't figure out how to manage any of her emotions. She had to force herself to do better and not let the nightmares and fears control her anymore.

In preparation of going out to eat with her mother, Bradley wore the most modest clothing in her wardrobe. She found a quarter-length sleeve, black top that flowed down past her bottom. Beneath it, she wore her one pair of jeans with no holes in them because, according to her mother, only deadbeats wore jeans with holes in them. Bradley placed a large bangle on her right wrist to cover her tattoos. Even though her mother knew she had the tattoos, it was best if she didn't see them. Lastly, she drew her hair into a bun, hiding the purple bits under the brown in her hair.

She arrived at the restaurant early and stood right outside. After brunch, she had to head into work for a few hours for their Sunday lunch rush. Thankfully, Jones had been understanding when she said she'd have to be a little late to go to brunch with her mother. He hadn't even asked why brunch was important.

"Bradley!" her mother called from the parking lot. Bradley walked over to her and gave her a hug. Her mother held on two seconds longer than normal before kissing her cheek. "You look lovely, dear. Where did you get that top? It really suits you."

"Um." Bradley glanced down at her top as she tried to remember. "I think I found it at a thrift shop. You've never liked my clothes before, has something changed?"

"What? Of course, I have. Now, come on. I'm starved."

They went inside and she followed her mother to the booth. Bradley tried to remember what she liked to eat here. She grabbed the menu and began looking it over, hoping for something filling.

"Now, Bradley, tell me what is going on with Vanessa. I know she talks with you."

Oh, Bradley thought. That was why her mother was being so nice; she wanted something. She lifted her eyes over her menu to look at her mother, who was staring back at her intently.

"I don't know what you're talking about, Mom."

The truth was Bradley had thought about going to her parents about Vanessa's behavior and what she knew about from all those months ago. But in the end, she decided against it. For as much as their parents loved Vanessa, they would only hinder her progress. They would either make it worse by not understanding or make it worse by saying something to upset her. Their parents had never really been the type to know how to deal with any sort of hard situation. They didn't tell them that their grandmother had died until two years later. Avoidance was often their tactic.

"Come on, now, Bradley. Ever since you two were little, you've been as thick as thieves. It's because of Grey, isn't it?" her mother asked. "Did he do something?"

"No." Bradley shook her head. "Grey loved Vanessa. He would never do anything to hurt her."

"Right. She's just been so unlike herself and missing brunch, again. Not like her at all."

"She's going through changes in life, is all," Bradley said. "You know her, she likes to handle it on her own. The best way any of us can help is by not making it a big deal."

"I don't make anything a big deal, Bradley," her mother huffed. "Honestly, you and Vanessa act as though I don't know how to behave myself when all I'm doing is worrying about my girls."

Bradley sighed. She reached across the table and took her mother's hand into her own.

"We're both fine, Mom. Really, we are. I promise."

"You're earlier than I expected," Jones said as he saw Bradley enter the bar. "What are you wearing?"

"I had brunch with my mom. I had to tone it down a little," she answered.

"Right. How was brunch?"

"Fine. She didn't say one backhanded comment to me or downgrade my appearance," Bradley mused.

"And that's strange?"

"Very strange."

Bradley walked around to the back of the bar to grab her apron and pad for orders. She would be serving tables today.

"Um, Mike?"

"What?" Jones said, looking over at her.

"Is that your name? Mike?" she asked. She wore a coy smile.

"No. We're doing that again?" he groaned. He couldn't understand her obsession with figuring out his name. No one had ever cared before now that he went by his last name.

"Yes. Branch?"

"That's a name?" Jones questioned, pulling a face.

"It is. I saw it on a baby name list last night while I was trying to think of what your name might be."

"It's definitely not Branch."

Bradley eyed him up and down.

"You're right. Basil?" Jones shook his head. "Bishop."

"So you were in the Bs last night?"

"Yes. Am I at least on the right letter?"

"No."

Bradley pulled a small pad of paper from her back pocket and began to mark some things off her list.

"Well, that narrows it down some."

"Why don't you stop guessing names and get to work? You've just had two days off."

"I know, I know," she bemoaned. "Back to work I go."

Jones had to admit, he missed having Bradley at work these past couple of days. He was starting to enjoy her company. She added a lightness to the business, always making it fun.

When the lunch rush ended, Jones divided out all the tips like he always did.

"What if we invited my sister to come tomorrow night?" Bradley randomly asked as she took her tip money from Jones's hand.

"I mean, sure, why are you asking me? It's an open bar. Anyone can come."

"Oh, I know. I was just thinking of ways to get her out of her house. She's basically becoming a hermit. That can't be healthy. So, if we invited her maybe that would help. She doesn't really like crowds though…"

"So maybe a bar isn't the best place?" Jones said, unsure. His mind went to Vanessa, and he doubted this was the best idea.

"I'd just have her arrive at opening. Maybe she could meet someone. Or you could talk to her," Bradley suggested.

"Me?" Jones pursed his lips in thought. "I will be working. And you will be too," he reminded her.

Bradley ignored him, tugging her hair down from her tight bun. Her dark locks fell down to her shoulders, allowing the purple to be seen again.

"You'd talk to her, wouldn't you? If she looked lonely?" Bradley bit down on the corner of her lip. "It's just that she needs to do something and I work evenings, so to get her here, she'd have to come where she knows somebody and—"

"Sure," Jones sighed, to get her to stop rattling on about it.

"Thanks. You're the best. See you tomorrow!"

Vanessa decided tonight she would make herself something to eat. For far too long, she'd been living off of freezer meals and take out. If she wanted to do better, she needed to put forth some effort.

She glanced through her refrigerator in hopes of magically finding something to whip up for dinner. It was nearly bare. She saw a half gallon of milk and some eggs. She lifted the eggs, opened them, and realized they were months old. Her nose squished up in disgust.

"Take out it is," she murmured to herself. Tomorrow, she would go grocery shopping after work.

Knock. Knock.

"Vanessa!"

"Bradley?" Vanessa headed to her front door and unlocked it, finding her sister on the other side.

"I'm taking you to dinner," Bradley said with a large smile.

"But don't you have to work?" Vanessa asked.

"Yes. You're coming to Lucky Ones for a few hours tonight. Dinner will be on me."

"No." Vanessa shook her head. "I'm not going to sit at a bar while you work. That sounds like torture"

"But you need to get out of this glum space you've put yourself in. Get out, see people, and experience life."

"At a bar?"

"You'll just come for the early hours before it gets too busy. I spoke with Jones about it yesterday. He said he'll make sure you don't feel lonely."

"Wait." Vanessa crossed her arms over her chest. "You discussed me with your boss and you planned this yesterday? If you knew you were going to bring me yesterday, why didn't you give me a heads up?"

"Too much time to come up with an excuse on why you couldn't do it."

Bradley had her there. Vanessa tried to find something to say, but she had no excuses. She was already in her pajamas.

"Now, come on. Let's pick out something for you to wear, and I'll do your hair."

"But—"

"You don't have to stay long," Bradley said, gently pushing Vanessa toward her bedroom. "Just eat dinner and then you can come back home."

"Here." Bradley popped a plate of food down in front of Vanessa.

"Thanks," Vanessa said, unamused. She grabbed the ketchup and poured some over her fries.

"I don't know how you can do it that way. Don't they get soggy?"

"It's the best part." Vanessa shrugged.

"Gross." Bradley noticed Jones walking over to greet her sister, so she nudged her quickly to whisper, "Tell me some male names."

"What?" Vanessa asked.

"Come on, give me one," Bradley said with exasperation.

"Oh, okay, um….Ronald?"

"Good one!" The moment Jones was over by them, Bradley guessed, "Ronald?"

"No."

"I'm sorry, what is this?" Vanessa asked, confused.

"Jones won't tell me his first name. I've been making guesses." Bradley gave a big smile. "Eventually, I will guess it."

"But how do you know he'll tell you the truth if you do?" Vanessa asked wisely.

"I won't," Jones answered.

"Yes, you will! You have to."

"No. I don't." He cleared his throat. "Vanessa, I hope you enjoy your food. Please let me know if there is anything else we can get for you."

"Thank you, I will."

"And you." He turned his attention to Bradley. "I better see you back behind the bar in five minutes."

Bradley slid into the seat across from her sister, placing her elbows up on the table.

"Do you think he likes me?"

"I don't know," Vanessa said. "I am not sure I'm the best one to ask those types of questions." She ate a few bites of her sandwich. "How long do I have to stay?"

"At least an hour," Bradley told her.

"An hour! You said I didn't have to stay long."

"An hour is not long. Stop being so dramatic." Bradley rolled her eyes. "I should probably get back to work, but if you get bored come order a drink. It'll be easier to speak with you over there. And, you know, you can also go up there and speak to other people."

"Bradley, I am not quite ready for *that*."

"I'm not saying to find someone to date, just make a friend. That's all."

Bradley found a fry with the least amount of ketchup on it to steal before walking back over to the bar. Now that she'd proven her worth, she did both bartending and waitressing at Lucky Ones. Though, she preferred staying behind the bar. People chatted with her more there.

"Are you sure this is what your sister needs?" Jones asked. He poured a shot of whiskey into a glass for one of their regulars walking in. He was eyeing her sister the entire time, a worried expression on his face.

"Yes? Why?"

"She doesn't look comfortable."

"She's fine," Bradley said with a shrug. "She has to get out of the house. And here, I can keep an eye on her."

"If you say so."

"I do."

"Have you always been this stubborn?" Jones asked, raising his brow.

"Yes, and I'll take that as a compliment."

Vanessa checked her watch. She'd only been here for thirty minutes. While she knew she could get up and just walk out, she also knew her sister wouldn't let her live it down if she didn't just stay thirty more minutes.

The corner where she sat was the quietest part of the bar. She could observe those around her, but still stay partly hidden away.

"Is this seat taken?" a man asked. He smiled, trying to pull out the chair across from her. Vanessa internally panicked.

"Um, yes," she lied. "My sister was sitting there."

"Oh." He frowned. His hand lingered on the side of the table and he leaned down toward her, making her increasingly uncomfortable. "But I haven't seen her. You've been here all alone. Is she late?"

"No," Vanessa said, trying to keep her voice from shaking. "She works here."

"Oh, so you do have time to talk." The man got even closer to Vanessa, making her heart race.

"She doesn't," a gruff voice said behind the man. Vanessa turned her head toward the voice to find Jones with a scowl on his face. He placed his hand roughly on the man's shoulder and shoved him out of the way. "Take the clues and go away."

The man threw his hands up in frustration before grumbling something under his breath and leaving the table. Jones offered Vanessa a warm smile.

"Are you all right? Some people don't get the hint."

"Yeah, I'm fine. Thanks," Vanessa said, sincerely.

"Can I get you anything?"

"No."

Jones glanced over to the bar and then back to Vanessa.

"Are you enjoying yourself?"

"Your bar is very nice," Vanessa said. Jones crossed his arms over his chest.

"That wasn't what I asked."

"Honestly, this isn't really my scene, but I came here to keep Bradley off my back."

Jones laughed. As he laughed, his entire body moved with him. His eyes lit up and he finished with a wide grin.

"She can be persistent."

The more time Vanessa spent around Jones, the more comfortable she felt around him. She knew he was safe; that he wouldn't hurt her or her sister. She fell back in her chair and glanced up at him.

"Are you ever going to tell her your name?" Vanessa asked.

"No."

"You know, I could find it searching the records for this place. Your full, legal names have to be on the documents." Vanessa winked, curling a stray hair with her finger.

"But you wouldn't do that or tell Bradley that, would you?"

"I don't know," Vanessa teased. "It would earn me some major cool sister points."

"But you don't really need those, do you? You are cool, aren't you?"

"Am I?" Vanessa chuckled at the thought. "I don't think I am. I did get a tattoo when I turned eighteen. I was trying to be rebellious or something like that, and I never told anyone. Well, until now. I guess I just told you."

"What type of tattoo?"

"A purple butterfly right on my right hip. I thought I was *so* cool, but then I just kept it covered up. The only other person to see it was my ex, Grey. No one else ever has." A shiver ran up her spine when she said that but she shook it away. Then she forced herself to smile.

Jones rose his eyebrows, smirking.

"So Bradley doesn't know this?"

"No," Vanessa answered honestly.

"But she has tattoos, you know she wouldn't judge you. Why didn't you ever tell her?"

Vanessa twirled her straw in her cup, thinking about this question. She found the answer wasn't as clear cut as it should be and shrugged her shoulders.

"I don't know. But since I've told you my secret, you should tell me yours. What's your name?"

Jones narrowed his eyes, then he shook his head.

"Oh, you're good. You almost got me with your story about your secret tattoo. Was this some plot with Bradley to get me to tell you my name?"

"No," Vanessa said, acting offended.

"Right. Well, it didn't work. I'm not telling you. I bet you don't even have a tattoo."

"I do," Vanessa said. "You don't have to believe me, but it's right here." She pointed to the spot on her hip.

"Uh huh." Jones wasn't convinced.

Not wanting to be seen as a liar, Vanessa pulled the edge of her pants down to reveal the tops of the butterfly wings. She snapped the pants right back into their place almost as quickly as she'd shown him the ink on her skin. She shot her eyes up at him.

"See."

"And your sister has no idea?"

"Nope. You can ask her about it. I'd be willing to bet she'll think you're lying."

"Want to place a bet on it?" Jones playfully asked.

Vanessa dug into her purse and pulled out a five.

"Five dollars?"

"Deal."

After the last customer of the night left, Jones did his usual splitting of the tips and handed them out to all his workers. It was one of their weakest nights as far as tips went for the crew, but it was only a Monday.

"So," Jones said casually when he handed Bradley her stack. "Your sister was telling me about the tattoo she got when she turned eighteen."

Bradley took the money, but kept her gaze on him.

"Are you high?"

"What?"

"My sister does not have a tattoo. She would never get a tattoo, even if her life depended on it. Do you know that my parents would keel over and die if they even heard rumors of their golden child having any sort of ink on her skin? Where do you even come up with this stuff?"

"I didn't. She told me. She showed it to me. It's on her hip."

"Uh huh. You're funny, very funny. Good night."

Bradley walked toward the exit and Jones followed behind her.

"You have to believe me," Jones said. "I have five dollars running on this."

Bradley paused at the door of her car, placing her hand on the handle.

"Oh, so you and my sister are playing some bet on me." Bradley rolled her eyes. "That makes much more sense. My sister would never get a tattoo. While I would think that it was awesome, I know her. She wouldn't do it."

"But—"

"What type of tattoo is this fictional tattoo?"

"Butterfly."

Bradley laughed even harder.

"Oh, so a basic white girl tattoo. Yep. You both did come up with a convincing joke, I'll give you that. Anyway, it's late and I would like to go to bed. Goodnight, Jones. And sorry, I'm going to have to say my sister won this round."

She got into her car and waved at him before she drove away, leaving Jones alone beside his bar. *Damn*, he thought. He owed Vanessa five bucks. Then he laughed and went inside.

CHAPTER ELEVEN

V anessa was deep in her work when she heard the clearing
of a throat. She looked from her computer to see her boss
standing in the doorway of her office. She immediately stood.

Her boss, Mrs. Wheeler, always wore a black blazer, black
skirt, and nude tights with her hair cut right at her chin in a
blunt, dark bob. In the ten years Vanessa had worked here, she
had never changed up her style.

"Yes? Can I help you, Mrs. Wheeler?"

"Could you come up to my office at half past twelve? I have
some things I'd like to discuss with you," Mrs. Wheeler said.

"Sure, absolutely. Is everything, alright?" Vanessa asked, her
stomach tightening.

"Yes. I'll see you at twelve thirty."

Mrs. Wheeler left Vanessa alone in her office to ponder what
this meeting could be about. Vanessa knew she'd struggled
lately, but she worked very hard not to let it impact her work. In

fact, she worked even harder at her job. It helped keep her mind off everything else going on in her life.

She checked the time. It was only ten. She had two and a half hours to sit here and worry. Two and a half hours to stress over if she was being fired. How was she supposed to focus on her job during that time?

Since she couldn't focus, she decided to take the elevator downstairs to the coffee shop. A nice cup of warm coffee would only make her nerves worse, but she couldn't think of anything else to fill the time. So she walked over to the conveniently placed coffee shop to grab something to drink and maybe something to eat, though she was sure she wouldn't actually be able to eat. Her nerves were too high.

When she reached her boss's office, she was told to wait in the chair by the door. Vanessa sat there, bouncing her knees up and down.

"Ms. Price? Are you coming?" Mrs. Wheeler asked.

"Oh, sorry." She stood. Before she walked in, she took a deep breath.

"Sit down."

Vanessa did as she was asked.

"As you know, Ms. Price, we are all over the country."

"Yes."

"And about six months ago, you asked for a transfer."

"Yes, but you said there weren't any opportunities," Vanessa said. She remembered that day clearly. She'd been determined to leave Savannah and start somewhere new, somewhere better. She'd been hoping to get away as far and as fast as possible.

"That's right. There weren't. However, we now have a job opportunity in New York City. You would leave in a month."

"Wait, what?" Vanessa breathed. "A month? New York City?"

"I know this is a lot to process. I am sure you have a lot of questions, which I will be happy to answer for you. We would need to know by the end of this week if you'd like to take this job opportunity."

"I'll take it," Vanessa said, surprising herself.

"Are you sure? We haven't discussed salary or living expenses?"

Vanessa chewed on the inside of her lip, but nodded.

"Good," Mrs. Wheeler said with a bright smile. "You've always been one of our best here, Ms. Price. You'll do many great things for our company in New York. I'll give you the packet with all the information. You can read over it and then come back tomorrow with any questions. I won't have you sign anything until I'm sure you have read that packet."

"Okay. Thank you."

Vanessa took the packet and held it firmly in her hands. This was what she needed. She needed an escape from this town—from this life.

"New York? The city?" Bradley asked, her jaw wide open.

"Yes," Vanessa said, shrugging her shoulders. She handed her sister a spoon for her ice cream. "Come on, let's go sit in the living room."

Bradley followed her sister to the couch, still in shock. Her sister had never shown any desire to move out of Savannah.

"You hate large cities. They stress you out," Bradley pointed out.

"It's a good opportunity. Better pay."

"New York's cost of living is higher. Will you even be able to afford a place?"

"They help subsidize my living," Vanessa explained. "I'll live in an apartment building across from the building where the office is. I only have to pay part of the payments. I also won't need a car, so I can sell mine."

"But is this really what you want, Vanessa?" Bradley asked.

"Yes," Vanessa said.

"Good," Bradley said. "I just want to make sure this is what you really want."

"Since when was that your job?" Vanessa countered. "You act as though I'm some child that can't make her own decisions. I am nearly thirty. I'm *your* big sister."

"Alright, alright," Bradley conceded, lifting her hands up. "If you're happy, I'm happy. Have you told Mom and Dad?"

"Not yet. I'm going to wait until dinner this weekend."

"Oh, right, Dad's birthday. I did take the day off work so I could be there. Maybe I should bring cameras. I think they'll be excited." Bradley could just imagine how thrilled they would be; their perfect child, getting a promotion.

"I hope so, though I'm sure Mom will be fretting about our monthly brunch. Do you think she'll try to fly up to New York every month?"

"Or worse, do you think she'll force me to go?" Bradley squished up her nose, not pleased at the thought.

They both laughed, but Bradley felt an immense feeling of sadness sweep over her. Throughout her entire life, her sister had always been there. Even when she went to college, she'd only been a few hours away.

"I'm going to miss you," Bradley said, feeling the tears coming.

"I'll miss you too, but this gives you an opportunity to travel. You've always liked the city."

"I have," Bradley agreed. "But it still won't be the same without you here." She took a bite of her ice cream. "What will you do with your house? This was supposed to be the home you started your family in." Bradley internally winced at stating that fact.

Vanessa and Grey picked the house together. In the breakup, he told Vanessa to keep it. Bradley didn't know how they'd divvied up the money since then. She'd never thought to ask.

"I know," Vanessa said with a sigh. "This was supposed to be our starter home. But it's not. I'm going to sell it. I should have sold it a while ago. For some reason, I held on to it. But I'm not going to keep it, not anymore. I'll sell it and maybe use the money I make for it in investing or something."

"You could always rent it out and keep it, in case you move back one day and want to start over."

"No." Vanessa shook her head. "Even if I did, I don't want to live here anymore." She wiped quickly below her eye. Then she looked at Bradley. "I know it seems like I'm running away from my problems, but I think this will be really good for me. It's a fresh start. A new beginning."

"I know it is," Bradley said. She reached over, giving her sister's hand a squeeze. "And you'll do great. I know it."

The next day, Vanessa signed her new contract. It was official. She was moving from her home town and starting somewhere new.

"Congrats," Mrs. Wheeler said, giving Vanessa's hand a firm shake. "As the packet said, you'll have two weeks off to figure out all you need for moving to New York. I'll give you a few extra days, so the sooner you get all your clients wrapped up here or given to other people, you are free to start your transition."

"Thanks, Mrs. Wheeler."

Vanessa walked back to her office. She had been sure that the moment she signed those papers she would feel an immense surge of relief. But she didn't. She felt like she'd made the worst mistake. How was she going to leave her family? Leave the only home she ever knew?

Before she could spiral into a panic attack, she dialed Bradley's number and hoped she was awake for the day.

"Hello?"

"Tell me I'm not making some terrible mistake," Vanessa said. "I just signed the paperwork."

"You're not making a mistake, Nessa. We talked about it last night. This is what you wanted. This is your fresh start. I'm flying up to New York with you. I'm going to help you move. You aren't doing this all alone."

Vanessa felt her heart settle down. She took a deep breath and let out a relieved sigh.

"Right. Thanks."

"You still haven't told Mom or Dad?"

"Nope."

"What about Grey?"

Vanessa chewed on the inside of her lip.

"Why would I tell him?"

"I don't know. Don't you think maybe you should?"

"What exactly would I say to him, Bradley? He's moved on. He doesn't need me saying anything to him," Vanessa said sharply.

"Maybe. He was in your life for a long time. He might appreciate if you let him know, but that's all I'll say about it."

"Thank you," Vanessa said. The last thing she wanted was her sister to keep pushing her toward Grey. What could possibly be accomplished by her telling him anything?

"You don't have a tattoo, do you?" Bradley asked a beat later. "You don't, right? This was some elaborate joke you and Jones played on me, correct? I mean, you would have told me if you've had a tattoo for nearly 12 years, wouldn't you?'

Vanessa bit on the inside of her cheek to keep from laughing too hard.

"No comment."

"Wait….no, you don't get to answer that way. I told Jones you didn't, but…Nessa, do you?"

"I need my five dollars. Tell Jones I'll be by later this week to collect my money."

"Oh my god, you do, don't you? You have a secret tattoo. Oh. My. God. Vanessa! Why wouldn't you tell me?"

Vanessa spun around in her chair.

"Is it really a butterfly?"

"No comment."

"You're showing me next time I see you. Why would you tell Jones that and not me? I'm your sister!"

"I don't know. It was just a silly thing. I have to go, but I promise I'll show you the tattoo and tell you all about getting it later." Vanessa hung up the phone before her sister could ask her any more questions.

Vanessa watched the cars cross the road, checking both ways. She was finally able to turn left and down the road to her sister's apartment. They would be traveling together to their parents' house for their father's dinner. Vanessa's stomach was a mess. It had been that way since she signed the paperwork saying she was moving to New York City. While she was excited about her new adventure, there was still a nagging feeling that this wasn't really what she should be doing.

Her parents would be thrilled. She was, once again, doing exactly what they wished of her.

"Hey," Bradley said, climbing into Vanessa's car. She held a small present in her hands.

"Oh, what did you get Dad?" Vanessa asked. "I got him a book."

"A tie. I couldn't think of anything original to get him. I thought of a book, but I don't know which ones he owns, so I decided on a tie. Dad could always use a new tie, I guess."

"Yes," Vanessa agreed.

"So, you're telling them tonight? Are you nervous?"

"A little bit. I think they'll be excited."

"Oh, they definitely will. Golden Child Vanessa with a brilliant promotion in the city!" Bradley stretched out her arms dramatically. Vanessa rolled her eyes.

"You do know this will make you their soul focus, don't you? Without me here to take half their attentions."

Bradley made a face, letting out a low, disapproving sound.

"Don't remind me."

"I am sorry," Vanessa said.

"Don't be."

They drove the half hour to their parent's house. Their father always wanted a low-key dinner for his birthday. He didn't even like to celebrate, but their mother insisted. So he would only do it with the four of them, at home, and no hubbub.

Vanessa steadied her breathing before stepping out of the car. She grabbed the present for her father and then followed behind her sister. They walked up to the front door and knocked. Her mother opened it almost immediately with a bright smile on her face.

"Vanessa! Bradley! Oh it's so good to see you!" She hugged them both before waving them inside. Their father stood further into the foyer, arms wide for a hug. He took them both into his arms and held them close.

"My girls," he whispered. "Thank you for coming to my birthday."

Their father always smelled of cinnamon. Vanessa inhaled the scent, taking her back to her childhood when she'd cuddle in his lap while he read her books before bed.

"Of course, Dad," Bradley said, kissing his cheek. He kissed hers back before turning to Vanessa. He placed his hand on her cheek, frowning.

"Your mother is right. You've lost too much weight." Vanessa swallowed hard, giving her father a tight nod. "Come eat, your mom has made a whole buffet of food."

Their mother always cooked more than enough food for a crowd whenever they came over for dinner. Today was not an exception. The dining room table was exploding with appetizers. Vanessa spotted pigs in a blanket, a charcuterie board, several dips, and a veggie plate.

"We're doing a spread tonight," their mother explained. "Your father's request. So grab whatever you want and we'll eat in the living room."

"You're joking." Bradley chuckled.

"No, I'm not."

"Mom, we've never been allowed to eat in the living room," Vanessa said.

"Sure we have."

"No, we haven't," Bradley argued. "The rule has always been to sit at the kitchen table, *always*."

"Well, I guess we've decided to change that rule," their mother replied.

Vanessa and Bradley met eyes over their mother's head. Every so often their mother would do this; try to change things up to appear more easy going. They both knew it would be short lived, so they might as well enjoy it while it lasted.

Once they all had their food, they went into the living room. Their mother had placed television trays all over the room. Vanessa touched one, curious how ancient they were. They looked old, yet Vanessa knew she'd never seen them in her life.

"Sit, sit!" her mother said.

They took their seats and ate their food. Even though the place they sat was unusual, the meal itself was the same. Quiet.

"Um," Vanessa began, after everyone had finished eating. "I have some news."

"Oh!" their mother chirped. "And what is that?" The way her mother's eyes dazzled made Vanessa sure she was hoping to hear she and Grey were back together.

"I got a promotion," Vanessa quickly said.

"Oh, Vanessa, it's about time they promoted you!" her father exclaimed. He reached over, patting her shoulder supportively.

"Thanks, yeah, um…with the promotion, I'll be moving to New York City." She glanced nervously between both of her parents, watching as their smiles faltered.

They looked to one another before returning their gaze to Vanessa.

"New York City?" her mother asked. "But why so far away?"

"It's where they need me," Vanessa answered, shifting uncomfortably in her seat. "It's a good promotion, a good raise. They even pay for part of my living expenses."

"When will you move?"

Vanessa turned to her father.

"Next month."

"Next month!" her mother gasped. "But that's too soon. What will you do with your house? And what about Grey?"

"I'll sell my house," Vanessa said, "and I don't know what you mean by 'what about Grey?' He and I are no longer together. He's dating someone new. I'm sure he'll find out through the grapevine that I left."

"It's just a pity," her mother murmured. "You both were *so* good together."

"Jan," her father said, raising his eyes at their mother. Her mother huffed, but did change the topic from Grey.

"What about Maggie's wedding?"

"Who?" Bradley asked, moving the television tray to the side of the couch so it could be out of her way.

"Your cousin, Maggie. Her wedding is in two months."

"I don't even remember a Maggie," her sister said.

"Sure you do! You girls used to all play together when you were younger."

"I'll fly down," Vanessa said. "I'll make it work."

"I still don't remember her."

Vanessa nudged her sister to stop it. It didn't matter if they did or did not remember their cousin Maggie. Their mother would still insist they attend her wedding.

"Well, I guess that will work," her mother sighed. "But New York. I mean, it's a great opportunity and we're so proud. I guess we just always assumed we'd get to keep you here with us."

"We're very proud." Her father winked.

Vanessa gave a tight, uneasy smile, glad the talk about New York and Grey were both over.

When the evening ended, Bradley gave her parents each a hug, wishing her father another happy birthday. Jokingly, he'd put on the red tie she gave him over his tee shirt and was still wearing it. She playfully tugged on it.

"Your mother and I were talking about coming by to visit you at work soon," her father said.

"At the bar?"

"Yes. We'd like to meet the guy who saved our little girl."

"Okay. You do realize it's a bar?"

"Of course, Bradley," her mother said, patting her arm. "But your sister said they serve lunch on Sundays."

"That's true."

Bradley and Vanessa said their goodbyes again.

"Do you really think they'll come," Bradley asked her sister as they drove away.

"I don't know, probably," Vanessa answered. "Jones did save you. It makes sense they want to thank him."

Vanessa's eyes kept straight on the road, but there was trembling in her voice. Bradley could see the whites of her sister's knuckles as they gripped the wheel.

"You don't have to go," Bradley whispered. "You can find another job. You can stay."

"There's nothing for me here," Vanessa said. Her hand swiped below her eye.

"I'm here. Mom and Dad are here. It's not too late to take it back."

Vanessa let out an incredulous laugh.

"I signed a contract. This is what I worked toward. I have worked so hard."

"I know," Bradley said. "But you can change your path. Like your book. You have other talents, Ness. It wouldn't be the end of the world if you just quit your job."

"Maybe not for someone like you," Vanessa replied. Her words were not harsh, and Bradley understood what she meant. Bradley had no problem changing from job to job or taking risks in life. It wasn't like that for Vanessa, who had always followed the path she'd been given from a young age.

CHAPTER TWELVE

"Do you like Broadway shows?" Bradley asked, flipping through the channels on the television of the bar to find the big game for a customer.

"No," Jones answered. "But we never really did the stage scene when I was growing up."

"Really? Never? Not one? We went every Christmas season to the show that came to The Fox Theater in Atlanta. Sometimes, we got to go to another show in the spring. It was our big family trip each year."

"Sounds fun."

"What types of family vacations did you have?"

"Um, we went to my grandmother's house for Christmas. She lived near the beach. But we never went when it was warm enough to enjoy the water," Jones answered.

"Never?" Bradley asked.

"No. We only saw her once a year."

"Oh," Bradley said. "Do you think you'd like to go to the theater some day?"

"I don't know, maybe."

"Now that Vanessa will be in New York, I was thinking of making it a bi-yearly thing. I'd go and visit, she and I would go and see some shows and the sights."

"Could be fun," Jones said. "Seems you're handling the idea of her moving better now."

"I am." Bradley nodded. "Maybe this is just what she needs. Here, everything is a reminder of her past. Running away might do the trick for her. Hopefully, she can find happiness in New York. And I don't mean a new man or anything like that, though I'll be happy for her if she does. Just happiness in her own skin. Maybe in New York she'll find her passion for writing again."

"She writes?" Jones's eyes lit up with curiosity.

"Yes, but she won't let anyone read it."

"What types of stories does she write?" he asked.

"It's a fantasy. She's so talented," Bradley gushed about her sister. "I only read some of it, but what I read was amazing."

"Hmm, interesting. So your sister is a creative type, like you. She writes, and you paint."

"Good memory."

"And what do you want to do with these paintings one day?"

"I don't know," Bradley answered. "I just do them for myself. I used to sell them at Farmer's Markets, but then I got too busy."

"Maybe you'll get back to it soon." His grin made Bradley's heart skip a beat.

Bradley felt a rush of blood move up to her cheeks. She ducked her head down and grabbed a towel from the drawer to wipe up a spill.

"Maybe."

She was drawn out of their conversation when she saw her parents walking into the bar. It was not a Sunday. It was not lunch. They'd arrived right before the rush at eight thirty.

"What?" she said beneath her breath. This was a surprise. She quickly made her way past Jones and toward her parents.

"Mom, Dad!" she greeted. She tugged on her crop top, hoping her mother wouldn't say anything about what she was wearing. "I didn't expect you tonight. It's late. Aren't you two usually in bed by now?"

"Oh, Bradley," her mother said, bending over to kiss her cheek. "Your father has tomorrow off, and I am retired. We aren't some old farts who can't have fun."

Bradley stared at her parents. She hadn't expected her mother's little 'change' to go this far.

"Is one of you dying?"

"No, don't speak in such a manner, dear," her mother said with a quick shake of her head. "Now, where is Mr. Jones? We want to thank him."

"Just call him Jones," Bradley said.

Jones stood over by the bar, cleaning one of the glasses. He wore his tight, blue shirt, making his tattoos and muscles prominent on his arms.

"Jones, these are my parents, Jan and Mitch. Mom and Dad, this is Jones."

Immediately, her mother's face brightened. She smiled and took Jones's hand while placing her other hand on top. She stepped even closer to him, her cheeks turning red.

"Bradley never told me how nice you looked."

"Mom," Bradley said, shocked.

"Jan, don't embarrass the young man," her father stepped in.

Bradley wished her sister was here to witness this moment. Vanessa would never believe their mother would have a crush on Jones. She struggled to believe it, and it was happening right in front of her face.

"Thank you," her mother said. "You just stopped that man from taking our little girl. Who knows what could have happened to her, had you not been there."

"I only did what any decent person would do," Jones answered.

"Well, we are grateful you were there," her father said.

"Do you both want to stay for dinner? We have a new double cheeseburger on the menu," Jones told them.

Internally, Bradley hoped they wouldn't stay. But externally, she smiled.

"Oh yes, we haven't eaten yet, have we Mitch?"

"No, we haven't."

"Great," Bradley said. "Why don't I find you a seat?"

She sat her parents and took their drink orders. Then she went to her phone to text her sister.

Mom and Dad just showed up at Lucky Ones. They're staying for dinner.

But it's after 6. Since when do they go outside after 6? Vanessa answered back.

Oh, and I think Mom has a crush on Jones.

What?!

Yes, I know. Gross. I got to go. Tell you about it later.

Bradley slid her phone back into her back pocket and got her parents' drink orders ready. When she took them over, she found Jones chatting with them again.

"I see you're getting along?"

"Of course we are, dear. Now, you don't have to entertain us. Go back to work. We'll just watch you."

"Well, that's not creepy or anything."

"Go on now."

Bradley wished she could stay nearby to see what Jones and her parents were talking about, but she did have to work. The bar was already filling up. It would only get more crowded over the next hour.

Vanessa wanted all the details about what was going on at the bar, but she knew her sister wouldn't be able to update her until later. She thought about throwing something on and pretending she'd just showed up, but she was already in her pajamas for the evening.

She walked into her office and decided to start going through her things. There was old paperwork she could throw away, some items that needed to be packed for New York, and some things that could be sold. She decided she'd start three piles on the floor.

First she looked at her books. She knew little about her apartment in New York, except that it would have a lot less room than her house did now. She'd have to either put a lot of these books into storage, sell them, or figure out a way to make it work in her new apartment. Her hand ran over the spines of the books. She'd never gotten rid of any of her books before.

She moved to another area. Books would come later. Right now, she wasn't in the right headspace to even think about getting rid of any of them.

She sat at her desk and opened the top drawer. Most everything in the drawer were stacks of paperwork. She went through each piece, sorting them into important and trash piles. Then she pulled on her bottom drawer, remembering it was locked. Vanessa stood to search for the key. Where had she put it?

"Right," she whispered. It was hidden under her desk. Her hand slid beneath, finding the hidden compartment and pulling out the lock. She unlocked the drawer and pulled out her manuscript. Her hand ran over the top. She stared at it for a long moment. Did she bring it with her to New York? But why would she?

She shook her head. She went and placed it on the table by the front door. She knew exactly where it needed to go and who it needed to go to.

A scream escaped her and Vanessa sat up, her hand over her chest. It took her a few seconds to realize she was at her house, alone. No one was here. She had been sleeping.

Vanessa took several deep breaths as she clutched onto the edge of her couch. Slowly, her breathing calmed, and she stood. She walked into her kitchen, grabbing a cup for water. On her kitchen counter, she saw the bottle of merlot she'd bought for a dinner party months ago that never had been opened. She pulled it toward her, holding the top in her hands.

She hadn't allowed a drop of alcohol to touch her lips in so long, but she got out her wine opener anyway and opened the top. She grabbed a glass and poured some wine. However, the moment the smell hit her nose, she felt sick.

Vanessa walked the bottle of wine over toward her sink and poured the liquid out. She watched as it emptied. When it was all gone, she placed it into the glass recycling bin under her sink. That's where she spotted the whiskey she'd bought for Grey. Every so often, he enjoyed a whiskey and ice.

The bottle was half full. Vanessa wondered if whiskey went bad after being opened for a certain amount of time. She grabbed it out and looked at the dark liquid. Sleep alluded her. She needed something to help her. The sleep aids no longer worked, so maybe this would.

Since she didn't have any soda in her house, she would have to drink it as is. Vanessa added some ice to her cup and then the whiskey. She took a quick, long gulp. Her face squished in disgust and she gagged. Yet, she continued to drink until it was all gone. Then she poured herself another, hoping it'd allow her to sleep all night long with no nightmares.

Bradley knocked several times on her sister's door the next morning, until she finally found the key to her house and unlocked it herself.

"Nessa?" she called out. She walked into the dimly lit house to find her sister sleeping spread out on the couch. Her neck was nearly off the edge, making Bradley wince as though it was her own neck in pain.

Bradley walked around to the other side and sat down by her sister, easing her head up and onto the couch. She gently nudged her shoulder.

"Vanessa?"

Vanessa grunted, hiding her head beneath her pillow. Bradley sighed and stood. Her eyes then fell to the coffee table where she saw an empty bottle of whiskey lying on its side. Bradley lifted it up, shocked.

"It's eight in the morning," Bradley said, raising her voice. "You're usually up by now."

"And you're usually not."

"Yeah, well I couldn't sleep."

"Just leave me alone," Vanessa answered. She drew the blankets up and over her head.

"I came to take my sister for coffee and to tell you about Mom and Dad visiting me at work last night. I didn't expect to find you hungover when I arrived."

Vanessa used her arms to drop the blanket from over her face and looked at her sister.

"I'm not hung over." But even though she insisted it, Bradley could see the redness in her sister's eyes and hear the gruffness in her voice.

"Oh, you're not?"

"No."

Bradley lifted the bottle up for her sister to see.

"And what is this? Who else was drinking with you, then?"

"It wasn't even full. I just had a little to take the edge off so I could sleep, is all. What's the big deal?"

Vanessa finally got herself off the couch and grabbed the bottle from her sister's hand. She placed it back down on the coffee table.

"I thought you were doing better," Bradley said, disheartened. Vanessa's arms crossed over her chest.

"I am fine," she stressed. "I'm an adult. I'm allowed to have a drink now and again."

"Then why don't you sleep in your bed? Or even the guest bed?"

Vanessa's lower lip came between her teeth before she shrugged her shoulders. She brought her hand up to cover her mouth, turning away from Bradley.

"I just needed to be able to sleep last night," she said quietly. "A lot is on my mind with the upcoming move. I need you to trust me."

Bradley stepped forward, placing her hand on her sister's shoulder and giving it a squeeze.

"You're my big sister. I always trust you. Would you like to grab coffee on the way to work and I can tell you about work last night?"

"Yes. That sounds great." Vanessa began to make her way toward her bedroom before she stopped. "Oh!" She went and picked something off the foyer table, and then handed it to Bradley. It was her manuscript. "I want you to have this. You may finish it, but you cannot show it to anyone else."

"You didn't throw it away." Bradley widened her eyes in surprise.

"Of course not. But really, for your eyes only. Promise?"

"I promise."

Chapter Thirteen

In just a few short days, Vanessa would be moving to New York. She still struggled to believe the time was nearly here. She'd packed up the belongings that would be traveling with her, but most would either be in storage or sold with the house. Her apartment in New York came fully furnished.

Tonight, however, she wasn't going to think about any of that. She was going to see her sister at work and just enjoy the evening. She stepped into the bar and spotted her sister pouring a line of shots for some girls dressed in bridal wear. She briefly wondered if this was a spot often frequented by bridal parties before taking a seat at a corner booth.

"Bradley didn't tell me you were coming tonight." Vanessa glanced up to see Jones standing beside her. He held a pad in his hand to take orders and there was a pen behind his ear. His beard had been freshly trimmed, and Vanessa found she liked it that way.

"Didn't tell her," Vanessa said. "I'm finished up with work until the move, so I thought I'd just stop by. She seems at home here." Again she looked at her sister, who was chatting away with the bride to be. Her smile was contagious, making everyone around her just as bright and cheerful as she was, even Jones.

His usual quiet demeanor seemed livelier, and his own lips curled into a smile. He glanced at Bradley and then back to Vanessa, pulling the pen out from behind his ear.

"Yes, she's become one of the regulars' favorites," he said. "Can I get you something to eat? Or drink?" He moved closer to her and as he turned the page on the pad, Vanessa could see his toned arm flexing against the opening of his white tee shirt. A weird sensation went through her and she quickly looked away.

"Um, a burger and fries, and a whiskey on ice."

Jones nodded, writing it down.

"I'll have to see your ID."

Vanessa leaned forward and tapped her finger on the table.

"You do know I'm older than Bradley." There was that lightness again. Around Jones—much like when she was around Bradley—she didn't feel nervous or anxious. The old Vanessa could shine for just a little while.

"I do, but the rules are the rules," Jones said, playfully raising his eyebrow.

Vanessa dug into her purse for her wallet and moved items around, unable to find what she needed. She never left home without her ID. Panic bloomed in her chest before she glanced up and gave an uneasy smile.

"Well, I guess I'm not getting anything. I must have left my wallet at home on my dresser when I changed out purses tonight."

"I thought you were the responsible sister," Jones teased.

"I know, me too," Vanessa teased back. She chuckled, tucking her hair behind her ear. "Maybe my sister will take pity on me and buy me a burger. Or wait! You owe me 5 bucks. I *told* you she wouldn't believe you."

"You did, you did." He rose his hands up in mock surrender. "Fine, it's on the house. Plus, I know you're old enough for whiskey. Your sister told me you'll be celebrating your 30th birthday when you move to New York. She said you guys are going to see a show."

"Yes, we are. I don't know which one, Bradley planned it all. It's a surprise. And you don't have to do that. I can get Bradley to cover the cost, and I'll pay her back."

"No worries," Jones said, with a wave of his hand. "It's on the house." He scribbled on his pad. "It'll be out shortly."

"Thank you."

In the middle of the table, Mads placed a trail mix of some sort for the patrons to snack off of while they awaited their meals. Vanessa picked around the mix for the chocolate chips and ate a few of them.

"That was changed out before you sat down, wasn't it?"

Her sister sat down in the chair across from her.

"Yes, it's a fresh bowl."

"Oh, good." She dug into the bowl to grab a few different things and took a bite. "Are you sure I don't need to pay for my flight?"

"Yes. It's all covered by the job. They pay for me plus one person."

"Nice. I'm excited. I've always wanted to go to New York. I've written us a whole itinerary of things to do that Saturday."

"That sounds fun," Vanessa said.

Jones walked back over, placing the whiskey she'd ordered down in front of her.

"You ordered whiskey?" Bradley asked.

"Yes," Vanessa answered with a quick shake of her head. "Am I not allowed to drink whiskey?" She stared her sister down, daring her to make another comment about her choice of beverage. She wasn't about to allow her little sister to make her feel ashamed of her choices. She had always been the levelheaded one. Her hand reached out for the glass, she lifted it, and took a long sip, never breaking eyes with Bradley.

"Of course not," Bradley said tightly. "You're an adult. You can do whatever your little heart desires."

Bradley huffed and got up from the seat to head back to the bar. Jones was still there, his eyes going between Vanessa and Bradley. He stood there for a moment and opened his mouth to speak before closing it, seemingly deciding not to get involved. Then he walked away.

Now that she was alone, Vanessa could nurse her drink without judgement. She had no plans on getting drunk. And even if she did, who cares? She'd spent way too much of her adulthood making sure she behaved perfectly. She was tired of it.

Bradley came back over about ten minutes later with Vanessa's food and her own basket of fries. She sat back down and grabbed the ketchup from her sister.

"I have a ten minute break," she said.

"Oh, nice."

"Are you enjoying yourself?"

"Sure," Vanessa replied. "I've grown a bit fond of this place."

"Really?" Bradley asked with a laugh.

"Really," Vanessa said. "Why?"

"I just never expected you to be fond of a bar."

"Well, you work here and Jones is here. It's not just any bar."

"No, I suppose it's not," Bradley said.

"I should probably go once your break is over," Vanessa said. "I have a few more things I need to get done before I move."

"You're fine to drive?" Bradley asked cautiously, trying to squash any bit of judgement from her voice.

"Yep. I only had one drink."

They sat with one another for a little while as they both munched on their food. Vanessa only ate about half of her burger before standing up, deciding it was time to go.

"Be safe. Call me when you get home. I love you."

"Love you too."

Vanessa blew her sister a kiss before walking outside. When she stepped into the street, she saw a shadow in the distance. The man stood far off, smoking a cigarette, his eyes on her. Vanessa tightened her hands around her keys. There was something familiar about the man. She quickened her pace. He moved forward. Her heart raced. But then he stepped under the street light. Vanessa realized he wasn't who she thought at all, and that he wasn't looking at her. He was on his phone, and his eyes looked out at a distance.

With a shake of her head, Vanessa got into her car and locked the door. Then she rubbed her temple. Maybe her sister was right. Maybe she was losing it.

Despite the man not being who she thought he was, Vanessa couldn't sleep. She tossed and turned on the couch until she finally gave up and turned on the television. All night she watched infomercials. Several times throughout the night, the advertising was so tempting that she found herself feeling like she needed whatever they were selling. One almost convinced her to buy some dog hair remover. She didn't even have a dog.

By the time the sun started to rise, she began to drift to sleep. She curled to her side and allowed herself to fall into her slumber, but her sleep was short lived. A knock came at her door a few hours later. She sat up, yawning.

Quickly, she walked to her front door, assuming it was Bradley on the other side, probably there to scold her for her one drink the night before. But when she snatched open the door, Grey was there.

Vanessa grew self-conscious, realizing she was wearing just a tank top and short shorts. Her hair was likely a mess, and she was sure her face looked like death. To combat this, she crossed her arms over her chest and gave a kind smile.

"Grey. What are you doing here? I didn't expect you."

"Sorry," he started, "I saw your mom this morning downtown at the farmer's market and she mentioned you were moving to New York. I just thought I would come by to say goodbye."

Vanessa felt tears welling in her eyes. She blinked them away.

"I'm sorry I didn't tell you. I should have. It's just—I didn't know what to say, I guess. You and Emma are dating. I didn't want to get in the middle."

"Right. Um, can I…"

"Yes, come in, come in," Vanessa said, waving him inside. She was glad her house was packed up, and so there wasn't much for a mess. She quickened her pace to the couch to clean it off, hoping he wouldn't notice she slept there the night before. Then she motioned for him to take a seat. He did. She followed after him.

"This is a big promotion for you. Are you excited? New York, wow," he said. His eyes were bright and he was clearly proud of her. "You'll do such great things there."

"I hope so," Vanessa replied. She grabbed her robe from over the back of the couch and slid it over her shoulders, covering herself better. "I am a little excited, a little overwhelmed. But this is a great opportunity for me and this job."

"What about your writing? Have you finished your first draft?"

"Oh, um…" She took in a steady breath. "No. I don't plan on pursuing that anymore."

"What? Why?" he asked. "What you showed me was really good. I'd hate to think you were giving all of that up."

Vanessa twiddled with the tie of her robe.

"I'm not giving anything up, Grey. I am pursuing my career goals."

Grey frowned. His hand reached forward, lingering above her knee before he pulled it back to his lap.

"One day, I hope you'll tell me what happened between us," he said quietly.

"I don't know what else there is to say," Vanessa lied. "But you seem happy, with Emma."

At the mention of his girlfriend's name, Grey visibly brightened. Vanessa's heart ached at the sight of him happy with someone else.

"I am," he answered. "Emma and I are happy."

"And does she know you're at my house?" Vanessa asked.

"No, but she won't mind," he answered. "She trusts me."

"That's good." Vanessa inhaled sharply. She stood, wrapping the robe tighter around her middle. "Is there anything you'd like from the house?"

Grey shook his head.

"You gave me everything back when you broke up with me," he reminded her.

"Oh, right." Vanessa tugged on her fingers, missing the time when she felt comfortable around Grey.

He stood.

"I'm sure you'll take New York by storm," he said, smiling sincerely. "You're always impressing everyone."

"I don't know about that, but thank you."

They stood there in awkward silence for a moment before Grey walked forward and placed his hand on her upper arm. He gave it a quick squeeze.

"Goodbye, Vanessa."

"Goodbye, Grey."

Jones found Bradley in the back of the kitchen, sitting on a small stool, and reading something. She was so immersed in whatever it was that she didn't hear him walk by. He glanced down, trying to get a peek.

"What are you reading?" Jones asked. Bradley didn't look up. "Bradley!"

She jumped, pulling earphones out of her ears and placing them on her shoulders.

"Sorry." She gave him a small grin.

"Listening to music and reading at the same time?"

"Yeah, I like to listen to classical music as I read. It helps keep me from getting distracted while I'm reading," she explained. She flipped the pages of the spiraled bound paper and covered the title with her hand.

When Jones saw she was being mysterious about the work before her, he pursed his lips.

"And what are you reading?"

"My sister's manuscript."

"What's it about?" Jones asked. He was even more intrigued now.

Bradley brought the manuscript up against her chest.

"I don't think I'm supposed to say. But I can tell you it's really good and it's a fantasy story." Bradley stood from the stool and hid the manuscript into her large bag.

"Oh?" he asked. He wanted to know more. Books, he knew. Books, he understood. Vanessa, he didn't know or understand, but maybe her book would give him more insight of the woman who sometimes came into his bar, who always looked on edge, but also offered him laughs and friendship.

"Yep."

"And why were you reading it here?"

"It's between shifts," Bradley said with a shrug. "I haven't been able to put it down. It's so good."

"Is she going to publish it?"

"No," Bradley answered. "There was a time when it was her dream, but she said she doesn't want that anymore. I stumbled upon it when I was staying at her place. She got really angry at me for reading it, but now she's forgiven me and gave it to me to finish reading," Bradley explained.

"Well, maybe she'll change her mind," he said.

He pondered Vanessa's book as they walked into the main area where Mads was already preparing for the dinner rush. Since it was a Saturday, they needed to be prepared for a busy night. Right as he went to grab the remote to change it to sports for the evening, Bradley snatched it from his hands. He furrowed his brow, but then noticed what was on the screen. He growled. It was Allen Carter.

Bradley turned up the volume.

More women have come forward against Allen Carter, saying he was the man who assaulted them. As the case mounts, it seems it will become more and more difficult for Carter to receive a not guilty verdict.

"It's good news," Jones said.

"Very good," Bradley agreed. "When I saw his face on the screen, I got scared. But more and more women coming forward is great. I can't see how he'll get away with it. You and Mads are witnesses, me, all those other women. It has to be a clear cut case."

"I agree." There was a sense of relief knowing there was a good chance justice would be served.

"Your story is literally insane! I can't believe it ends like that," Bradley said the moment her sister opened the door. Vanessa yawned, bringing her hand up and over her mouth.

"Bradley, it's five in the morning."

"I know. I opened up the book as soon as work finished and read until I got to the end. Vanessa, you have to write part two and you have to get this published, out in the world! Your story…it's beautiful!"

"Um, thanks, I think. I still don't know why you had to tell me so early. You could have come later in the day."

Bradley shrugged, walking past her sister and into her home. It felt a bit surreal entering her sister's home with so many boxes lined up along the hallway. She ran her fingers over the tops of some and sighed.

"I'm going to miss you. Soon I won't be able to just stop by and see you whenever."

"Right now, that sounds like a very good thing. Honestly, Bradley, the sun isn't even up yet."

"I know, I know, but we need to talk about this story of yours. What comes next? What happens to Rosina and Malik?"

Vanessa rubbed her temple, yawning again.

"I don't know," she said.

"You have to know! You're the writer!"

"Why are you so loud?" Vanessa cringed.

Bradley stepped further into her sister's house, where she found two empty whiskey bottles sitting next to the sink. She lifted one of them up, her heart sinking.

"How much have you been drinking?"

"Not much. Those have been from several nights. Not that it is any of your business, at all."

Bradley turned the whiskey bottle in her hands. It was a large bottle; one someone bought for a party, not to have for themselves. She looked at her sister, who wore a guilty expression on her face, but quickly tried to cover it up with a neutral look and a shake of her head.

"You don't have to be ashamed," Bradley said. "I'm not going to judge you." She treaded carefully. "If you feel you need to drink at night, I understand. You've been pushing down a lot. It's hard to manage trauma like that."

Vanessa slowly inhaled and exhaled before walking up to her sister and taking the bottle away from her.

"It's just a lot of stress, is all," Vanessa said, using her same excuse from before. "I'm not hiding anything from myself."

"I wish you'd speak with someone," Bradley tried, knitting her brows. "I want you to be okay. I want you to be happy."

"I am happy." Vanessa's voice came on a bit too strongly. "I'm moving to New York! I got a promotion at work! What is there not to be happy about? Do you think I should work some dinky bartending job like you do?"

"Hey," Bradley said lowly, jutting out her jaw. "Not everyone can be perfect like you."

"And it kills you, doesn't it? Not being the favorite child? Not amounting to anything?"

"I'm leaving." Bradley turned on her heel and headed straight to the front door. She grabbed the doorknob and turned it, expecting her sister to rush behind her. But she didn't. Bradley stood there for a moment before glancing back for Vanessa. Her sister was still in the kitchen, turned away from her.

When she realized her sister wasn't going to apologize or say anything else, Bradley left her sister's house.

Chapter Fourteen

I t had been four days since Vanessa had spoken to her sister, making this the longest Vanessa had ever gone without speaking to Bradley. The old Vanessa never would have said anything so degrading and horrible to her sister. She didn't believe a word that had come from her mouth, but she let them slip anyway. It was up to her go to Bradley apologize, but she hadn't, because then she'd have to admit Bradley was right.

Tonight they were meeting up for her birthday dinner and tomorrow they were supposed to be leaving together for New York City. How was she supposed to expect her sister to come along with her after the way she'd treated her? At every turn, she kept screwing up.

Her body felt dazed, detached from everything going on around it. It was as though she'd gotten onto a ride she couldn't get off. There seemed to be no escape in sight. She kept telling herself that what she did next would make her feel like herself

again, but nothing worked. She felt more and more disconnect-
ed with each change.

She met her eyes in the mirror, tugging her hair into a small,
low bun for dinner. She inhaled.

"It's time to get yourself together," she whispered to herself.

When she arrived at the restaurant in the Uber, her parents and
sister were already there, standing on the outside patio. Her
father spotted her first, waving her down. Then her mother
smiled, reaching her arms out for a hug. Bradley only gave her
a tight smile, not saying a word.

They walked inside and were taken to a booth near the back.
Her parents slid into one side, meaning she and Bradley would
have to sit in the other. Vanessa pointed to let Bradley go first,
but Bradley remained in her spot.

"You first," Bradley said, crossing her arms tightly over her
chest. "I hate sitting on the inside."

"Fine," Vanessa bit. She slid in, grabbing the menu so she
wouldn't have to talk to anyone. Her sister slid in beside her,
almost too close, making Vanessa hit the wall beside her. She
lifted the menu higher.

"Are you all ready for your move? Do you need your father or
me to do anything with the house after you've left tomorrow?"
her mother asked.

"No, my realtor has the keys. She's taking over all offers for
the sale. A cleaning crew comes on Monday to do a deep clean.

I think I have everything settled." Vanessa kept her head behind the menu.

"We've decided we'll come up for Christmas," her mother said. That got her attention. She dropped the menu.

"What?"

"The city is supposed to be beautiful during Christmas time. We'd get a hotel, maybe do some sightseeing, and celebrate Christmas."

"Um, sure, why not," Vanessa said, trying to hide her disappointment.

"What about me?" Bradley asked.

"You'd come with us, wouldn't you?" her mother asked.

"I guess, but what if I have to work?"

"That's months from now. You have time to figure that out," her father said. "Vanessa, we thought you'd be thrilled."

"I am. I just had been thinking about Christmas at home and coming home for the holidays, but this will be nice. Fun, truly."

She hid her face back into her menu. What she wouldn't give for some hard liquor right now. But with her parents and sister sitting near her, she'd have to settle for a glass of water. She missed being able to handle the smell of wine, because at least that could take some of the edge off.

"What time do you want your father to take you to the airport tomorrow? Is your flight at 1?"

"Yes," Vanessa answered. Her mother began to count backwards with her fingers.

"He should probably pick Bradley up at 10 and you up right after."

"Mom, that will have us at the Savannah Airport nearly two and a half hours before our flight. We will not need that much time," Bradley said.

"It's better to be there too early than not early enough," her father said. "You don't want to miss your flight."

That nagging voice inside of Vanessa's head grew louder, causing her stomach to twist in anxiousness. *You have no idea what you are doing. You'll always remain on this train of nothingness.*

Bread and butter were dropped off at the table. Vanessa reached for a piece right at the same time as her sister did. They met eyes. Bradley turned away before Vanessa could read whether her sister was still angry with her or not. She placed the bread on her plate and began buttering it. Then out of nowhere, Vanessa decided to spread some butter on her sister's hand.

"Hey!" Bradley yelled. Vanessa bit her lip, meeting her eyes again. Bradley's eyes lit up. She reached over to Vanessa's cheek and rubbed the buttery hand against it.

"Girls! Girls! Seriously! You are too old for this behavior!"

But Vanessa just laughed. She and her sister were all right again.

"Why don't you sleep over at my place?" Bradley offered, after the sisters left the restaurant and got into Bradley's car. "You can grab your luggage and just stay with me."

"Or you could stay at the hotel with me. It's already paid for by the company. And it's nice."

"Yeah? How nice?"

"Nice."

"Okay, let's stay there."

Vanessa adjusted in her seat before reaching over to touch her sister's hand.

"I'm sorry for what I said. I didn't mean it."

"I know you didn't," Bradley said.

"And you…" Vanessa twisted her lips. "You were right, about the drinking. I'm not going to drink anymore. It was a stupid way to cope with, well, everything."

"Oh, Ness," Bradley murmured. "You're not stupid."

Vanessa rose her brow.

"I never said I was stupid, just my choice was."

"Well…" Bradley playfully started.

They both grinned.

"I really am sorry," Vanessa repeated.

"I know. It's done now. Now we get to celebrate you turning 30 and moving to New York!"

Vanessa groaned. Thirty.

"What? Aren't you excited?" Bradley asked.

"I don't know, maybe? I am excited about the move. It's a fresh start. I'm not as excited about turning 30."

"Why not? You're about to take New York by storm, Ness!"

Vanessa smiled. She was grateful for her relationship with her sister; that they were close enough for the fight to just fade away and no longer be a dark cloud over her head.

"Yes, I will."

After they arrived in New York, they took a taxi to Vanessa's new apartment. As they rode through the city, Vanessa sat back and watched as they passed each building. Her stomach flipped in excited anxiousness. This was her new home. The tall buildings surpassed her expectations, making her chew on the inside of her lip. It all seemed overwhelming, and yet a bit exciting. She hoped this would help turn her life around in a positive way.

When they reached her apartment building, she stepped out of the taxi and glanced up. She tried to count the floors, but she lost count around twelve. Her sister wrapped her arm around her shoulder, looking up with her.

"Here starts your new life."

"Yes," Vanessa agreed.

They were taken to the tenth floor to her apartment and given a key. The man told her to call down if she had any questions. Vanessa unlocked the door and went inside, placing her luggage down. Right before her was a small kitchenette and a little living area with a black couch, chair, coffee table, and a television attached to the wall. She made her way over to the large window behind the couch. There were buildings and buildings as far as her eyes could see, with specks of people rushing around below. She let out a long breath. This was it. This was her new home.

"This is nice," Bradley said, walking up behind her. "You get to have all of this for free?" Vanessa could hear her sister going through drawers and cabinets in her kitchenette.

"No. I pay some rent each month, it's just not the full rate."

"Wow," Bradley said. "Maybe I should have taken college more seriously. Those two weeks I was in college won't get me here."

"You like your life, though." Vanessa went over by her sister, curious to see what all her new apartment had. The kitchen came with some pots and pans, as well as dishes.

"I'm thinking of cutting my hair. Get rid of the purple, just be brunette for a while."

"Really? I can't remember the last time your hair was its natural color. Why are you wanting to do that?"

"A change, I guess."

"Is it for Jones?" Vanessa playfully nudged her with her shoulder.

"No, for me. I don't think he cares a bit about how my hair looks. I'm also not sure he likes me. Not like that, anyway," Bradley mused. She ran her fingers through her hair, staring at her purple ends.

"What makes you say that?"

"Oh, I don't know. He doesn't try to flirt with me or anything."

"It's because he's a good guy, Bradley," Vanessa said. "He isn't like the men you've dated in the past."

"What's that supposed to mean?" Bradley asked, with a laugh. "I know, I know. I've dated all losers."

"Not all of them. Um, Jasper, was that his name? He was cool."

"Nessa, I dated Jasper when I was sixteen. You're saying the only good choice I ever made was when I was a teenager?"

They both burst into laughter. Vanessa brought her sister over to the couch and they sat down. It made a loud pop sound and then a creak. The cushion was both too hard and too soft at the same time.

"I guess this is the downside to included furniture," Bradley said, running her fingers over the pleather material.

"I'll have to look into a new couch. I hope the bed is more comfortable." Vanessa jumped up, heading back into the bedroom.

With her fingers, she tested the edge of the mattress.

"Hmm."

Bradley went straight for it, rushing past Vanessa and jumping onto the mattress head first. She landed on it with her arms and legs spread out before turning over to face her sister.

"I think it's comfortable."

Vanessa twisted her hands in front of her. This was a new bed—an untarnished bed. She inhaled slowly and then sat down beside Bradley, bouncing lightly on her bottom.

"Will you actually sleep on it?" Bradley asked her, pulling herself up onto her elbows.

Vanessa acted as though she had no idea why her sister would ask her such a thing and walked over to the comforter set and sheets she'd bought.

"Help me make the bed."

Chapter Fifteen

After just three weeks at her new job, Vanessa was already in a routine. She thought there would be some learning curves and that she may struggle to figure it all out, but that had not been the case. She settled in just fine. Every day, she woke up, went to work, came home, and started all over the next day.

"Vanessa!" a voice called out, right as she stepped onto the elevator. A woman with dark red hair stepped on after her, breathing heavily. Vanessa tried to remind herself what this woman's name was.

"Um, yes, um…" She inwardly cursed herself. She'd just worked with her on a project last week.

"I'm Erica. I know. I'm also horrible with names."

"Yes, I'm sorry, Erica. Can I help you?"

"The girls and I were talking about doing a welcome night out with you. We've hardly gotten to know you, and you're new to the City. We could take you out for dinner and drinks."

"Um," Vanessa said, biting down on the inside of her cheek. "I don't know. That seems like such a big deal for just little ol' me. Surely, you don't want to waste a whole evening getting to know me."

"Sure we do! Our apartment building has a bar downstairs, then we can go to some of the other bars nearby."

"O-okay, sure. That sounds fun," Vanessa replied. She had told herself she was going to make a life for herself here in the city. Part of that would need to be making friends and having a life outside of her job.

"Good! Let's say Friday around eight we can meet up."

"Eight?" Vanessa still couldn't wrap her head around the later nightlife here.

"Is that too early? We could shoot for nine."

"No, eight sounds good. Can't wait."

Bradley's shorter locks still surprised her when she ran her fingers through her hair. She'd chopped off several inches, making it hit right below her chin. Even though she'd said she was going to keep her hair one color, she hadn't been able to stick with it. Just one day after getting it cut, she added one thick stripe of blue on the right. If she pinned back some of her hair, she could cover most of it up before meeting with her parents.

Today she was doing just that. Since Vanessa had moved, her mother asked her to meet more often. Bradley knew Vanessa used to speak to their mother daily on the phone, but for some reason, her mother wanted to see her in person almost every week.

She twisted and pinned her hair, covering as much of the blue as possible, and then dressed in her most modest clothing.

A knock came at the door.

"Coming!"

She rushed to the door and opened it to her mother standing on the other side. Her mother's eyes peered into Bradley's studio apartment, the judgement palpable. She curled her upper lip while narrowing her eyes.

"That's an interesting way to organize your pots and pans."

"Mom, they're just drying. I don't have a dishwasher," Bradley said. She let out a sigh. Seemed her mom was back to her usual self. That seemed about right on schedule.

"Oh, right, of course. And your hair!"

Bradley touched her hair. "Oh, yeah, what about it?"

"It's different."

'"Yeah, I cut it. Where's Dad?"

"Downstairs, looking for parking. Are you sure this is a good place to live, Bradley?" her mother asked.

"Mom, I've lived here for years. I thought you came over just to spend some time with me, not judge where I live."

Her mother grumbled before adjusting her shoulders and forcing herself to smile.

"Of course, darling. We just want to spend time with you."

For dinner, Bradley had set up her table with a small table cloth and brand new chairs. Her old ones had been falling apart, so having her parents come over gave her the excuse to buy new ones.

When her mother took a seat, her eyes roamed back around the room.

"It is quaint. Do you like it?"

"I *love* it."

"You don't want to move somewhere bigger? With more room? What if you get married? And want to have kids?"

"Well, none of those are in the plans for right now, so I am happy right here. It's my home."

Her father came in a moment later, holding a cake in one hand and some wine in the other.

"What's this?"

"I like cake," he simply said. She took the two items and placed them on the small kitchen counter space she had.

"We're not celebrating something?" Bradley asked.

"No," her mother answered. "What are we having for dinner?"

"Right." Bradley pulled out her phone from her back pocket to check the delivery time. "Food was supposed to be delivered by now."

"Oh, take out?"

"I don't really cook," Bradley said with a shrug. "There isn't much space."

"I'm sure whatever you ordered will be good," her dad stated with a grin.

Thankfully, the food arrived just a moment later. She sat it down on the small table and opened the containers. Her mother made mention about the type of food she'd chosen, but Bradley ignored her.

When she sat back down and began to eat, her mother paused her by placing her hand on her wrist.

"Tell us about Vanessa."

"Huh? What do you mean tell you about Vanessa? She's in the Big City. She has her new job. What is there to tell?" Bradley said, annoyed. She should have known her parents came for information, not just to spend time with her.

"I thought this big move was going to change everything, but she's withdrawing from me, Bradley. She hasn't spoken to me once on the phone and only texted me back a handful of times."

"Mom, she has a brand new job. It's probably demanding of her time."

Her mother's hand withdrew from Bradley's arm. Her mother tapped her fingers on the edge of the table twice and shook her head.

"Something has been going on with her. I don't understand why you won't tell me what it is. *You* are her sister."

Bradley took in a deep breath, giving herself a moment to respond. She thought of her sister up there in New York. Vanessa seemed just fine when they'd spoken on the phone, but maybe she was actively avoiding her mother's calls. Bradley couldn't blame her. It was much more difficult to avoid their mother while living nearby.

"She's busy," Bradley said, once more. "Vanessa has plenty on her plate. Plus, she'll be back in just a few weeks for the wedding. You really shouldn't worry so much about her."

"Alright, if you say so," her mother said. "She's just up there all alone."

"I'm sure she's fine," her father told her. He kissed her temple.

"Yes," Bradley said. "Now, why don't we dig into this cake?"

The lights of the city were hard to get used to. No matter how many lights Vanessa turned off in her home or how she adjusted her curtains, some light always got into her apartment. It was nearing midnight. She opened up the curtains, seeing the various lights surrounding her. Her free hand touched the glass and a small, shuddering breath escaped. It was beautiful, striking.

She could stand here for hours. Looking down below made her feel a myriad of feelings: excitement, loneliness, hope, sadness, joy. As she was adjusting to her life here in the city, she found her emotions all over the place. While she was excited about her new opportunities, she still missed home.

Her phone vibrated in her robe pocket and she dug it out, seeing a new text from her sister. With Bradley's schedule, Vanessa received messages at random times throughout the night.

I know it's late. Hope this doesn't wake you. Just checking in. Love you!

Vanessa read over her sister's words a few times before placing it back into her pocket, making a note to text her back in the morning. She knew if she texted now, her sister would want to talk. Talking could last for hours and she really should get to bed soon.

Just as she thought about her bed, she yawned. Her hand came up above her head. She closed the curtain and turned, and her eyes caught sight of her laptop turned on. She stepped forward to shut it. Though, before she could, she saw she had a notification on her social media page.

Vanessa plopped down onto her seat and clicked on the notification. The moment the picture popped up on her page, she froze. The notification had been a memory reminder. Above the picture said two years ago. Her eyes grew misty as she stared at the photo of her and Grey. They were facing one another, bright smiles on their faces, his hand cupped her cheek.

Quickly, Vanessa closed the laptop. It was time for bed.

When her shift ended, Bradley rubbed her eyes with her palm. She was exceptionally tired this evening. She had worked eight days straight. Tomorrow, she planned on sleeping all day and then going to bed early since she didn't have to work that evening.

As Bradley was heading toward the door to leave, she paused. She had an exciting thought—a possible idea. Her lips curled up slightly and she turned back around. Jones was the last person in the bar, refilling the ketchups for tomorrow's shift.

"My cousin has a wedding in a few weeks and if I don't bring a date, my parents will inevitably try to set me up with someone," Bradley started, her heart racing in her chest. "Um, so, do you think you could come with me?"

He glanced at her, not speaking for several seconds. Bradley swallowed hard.

"Like on a date?" Jones finally asked.

"Um, in the sense that you'd be my date for the wedding," Bradley said, chewing on the inside of her cheek. She held her breath, waiting for his response.

"When is it?" He closed the final ketchup and slid it over next to the other ones before wiping his hands with a cloth.

"Three weeks from Saturday."

"Hmm," he said. "I guess I could trust Mads to oversee Lucky Ones that night. Sure, I think I can make it work." He smiled at her.

"Awesome. I'll get more details and then text them to you," she said before exiting the bar. She wanted to leave before giving him a chance to change his mind.

The moment she stepped outside, she sent Vanessa another message.

Jones is coming with me to the wedding. Call me tomorrow to discuss. Ugh! I wish you were awake now.

Bradley shook with excitement. She climbed into her car and giggled. As she turned on her car, her phone immediately started to ring.

"Why aren't you asleep?" Bradley asked her sister.

"I was just about to go to bed when I saw your text. How exciting! How did it happen? Did you ask him? Did *he* ask you? Do tell!"

"I asked him." Blush creeped up Bradley's cheeks and she was glad she was alone in the car. "Just casually asked. I didn't want to make it this whole big thing."

"Right, of course."

Her sister's enthusiasm brought a smile to her face.

"So I just asked him and he said, 'sure, I think I can make it work.'"

"I know you're thrilled. You're finally going on a first date!"

"Well," Bradley said, "I'm not sure it's a date–date."

"Oh, I say it is. How exciting!!"

"Will you be bringing a date?"

"No," Vanessa chuckled. "Who would I even bring?"

"Well, I'm glad you're coming. I've missed you."

"I've missed you too. I just—" Vanessa stopped mid-sentence. For a moment, Bradley thought the line went dead.

"Ness?"

"I'm here. Sorry, I yawned. I'm exhausted."

"Maybe you shouldn't be up so late then."

"I know, I know. It's just hard adjusting to the sounds and lights in New York. I've tried some white noise on my phone, but I need to invest in some black out curtains. And I really should be sleeping. I'm going to pay for it when I go out tomorrow, well, tonight now, with the girls."

"Oh?" Bradley asked, surprised. "You're going out?"

"Yes, don't sound so shocked," Vanessa said, yawning again.

"I'm just happy for you. I'm glad you're going out. You're going to have so much fun."

"I think so. I should go. I'm about to fall asleep. Goodnight. Love you."

"Goodn—" The line cut off between them.

Bradley entered the parking lot of her building. She went into her apartment, locking the door behind her. After she dropped the phone on her table, she pulled her hair out of the two tiny buns on top of her head. Her fingers combed through her hair, allowing all the locks to fall over her face. She fell back onto her bed, letting out a pleased sigh.

She was going on a date with Jones. Giggles left her and she kicked her legs. She was going on a date with Jones!

Chapter Sixteen

Vanessa applied a darker shade of red over her lips, per her sister's instruction. She blotted it with a tissue and then glanced back at her phone screen for Bradley's approval.

"Yes! The red! Oh, Nessa! You look great," Bradley said through the screen. Vanessa tucked her stray hair behind her ear and looked back in the mirror.

"You really think so?" She tried to button the top button of her shirt, but it kept popping back open.

"You look beautiful, Ness, and leave that button undone. If you button that top one, you'll look like a nun. Aren't you going out for a night on the town?"

With a dramatic sigh, Vanessa dropped her hand from the top button.

"Fine."

"So, who all are you going out with?"

"Um, there's Erica. She's the one who invited me. And I honestly don't know the other girls' names," she said, making a face. "I am trying to learn them all. I believe there's a Rachel?"

"How are you so bad at names?" Bradley teased.

"It must be the getting old," Vanessa playfully said back. "So I look all right?"

"Yes, of course. Have fun."

"That's the plan."

"Okay. Go! Have fun! Text me when you're back in your apartment tonight."

Vanessa raised her brows.

"Worried about me?"

"Only in a way a sister is worried about her sister. Now, go! Love you."

Vanessa laughed.

"I love you too."

She hung up the phone and placed it into her purse before picking it up. As she stepped outside of her apartment, she was surprised to find one of the girls walking down the hallway. Her mind tried to recall her name.

"Vanessa!" The girl called out, rushing her steps to be next to her. She brought her arm around Vanessa's, making Vanessa pull back.

"Sorry!" the girl said. Vanessa let out a shaky breath, while hating herself for having such a reaction. She gave the girl a smile.

"It's fine. I just—I'm not a fan of being touched."

"Oh," she said. "I just live a few apartments down so I thought I might come to yours and go downstairs with you."

"Right. Remind me of your name?"

"Rachel."

"Right! Rachel. Sorry, I suck with names." Vanessa gave a bashful smile. Next to her, Rachel nodded and smiled back.

"You do have many more names to remember than we do."

"Yeah, but I think I'm getting the hang of it," Vanessa said.

The elevator doors opened to reveal the ground floor. Right as she stepped outside, she found the rest of the girls standing there ready to party. Their faces lit up upon seeing Vanessa and some of them squealed in delight.

"Well, come on," Erica announced to the group. "Let's get started."

Vanessa was enjoying the evening. Everyone was nice and she was finally getting everyone's name down. There was Rachel, Erica, Michelle, Tabitha, Laurie, and Sara.

Since she'd promised her sister she was not going to drink alone anymore, she'd avoided all forms of alcohol, but tonight was proving to be more difficult to do so. She had been able to evade alcohol at their first stop downstairs, but by the time they headed to the bar down the block, Rachel bought everyone a shot.

The shot sat in front of Vanessa as everyone else held theirs up in front of them. Erica noticed, nudging the shot glass closer toward her.

"Drink up, Vanessa! Come on!"

With a bated breath, Vanessa lifted the glass up to her mouth and downed the liquid. It went down smoothly. Everyone around her cheered.

"Another!"

"No," Vanessa said. "Just the one for me."

"Do you not drink?" one of the girls asked.

"I do." Vanessa didn't want to lie. "Sometimes, but not often."

"Okay," Rachel said. "That's cool."

Vanessa let out a sigh of relief. She sat back in her chair and watched as the girls downed another shot of liquid. She asked for a water and slowly sipped on it. When she wasn't drinking the liquid, she kept her hand over the top of the cup. Around her, her co-workers continued drinking, and eating very little at the same time. Vanessa observed Erica tripping over her foot and catching her balance by nearly knocking down another of the group. Everyone laughed.

"Erica, maybe you should sit down and eat something," Vanessa said. She got up from her seat and helped Erica into her own barstool. There was a small bowl of pretzels on the bar which Vanessa grabbed and placed into Erica's hands. "Eat."

"Oh, let her have fun." Someone tugged on Vanessa's shoulder. Vanessa tensed, turning around toward the sound of the person. She expected one of her co-workers, but instead it was a guy she didn't know.

"Don't touch me," Vanessa warned. She took a step back, suddenly feeling overwhelmed in this situation.

"Vanessa, he's just some guy. Come on, sit down, have another drink. You need to loosen up," Rachel said. She was slurring her words. Vanessa glanced around at the group. She was the only one who was sober.

A drink got shoved into Vanessa's hand. She didn't even know who had given it to her. Her eyes glanced down at the dark liquid that bubbled at the top.

"Where did this come from?"

"The bar. I ordered two drinks. Just drink it," one of the women said.

"No." Vanessa sat it back on the bar. "No one should drink it. Has everyone been watching their drinks? You never know what—"

Her waist was grabbed by someone, making Vanessa nearly jump out of her skin. She screamed. Everyone laughed, including the guy behind her. She turned, slapping his chest. It was the same guy from before.

"I told you not to touch me!" she yelled. The guy ran his fingers through his long, blond locks and smirked, not at all turned off by Vanessa's state.

"What is *wrong* with you?" Rachel asked. "He's just teasing."

Harsh breaths left Vanessa's lips. Tears stung her eyes. Was she overreacting?

"I should go," Vanessa said. She bent over to grab her purse before rushing out of the bar. Tears began to spill from her eyes the moment the fresh air hit her face.

"Vanessa! Vanessa!" someone shouted at her. Vanessa continued to rush down the sidewalk, not sure where she was heading. "Vanessa! Stop, please!"

Vanessa stopped her steps and finally turned. Erica stood a few feet away from her with her hands up in surrender.

"I'm sorry," she said.

Vanessa wiped the tear from under her eye.

"I doesn't matter. I-I overreacted," Vanessa said.

"I don't think you did," Erica disagreed, taking a cautious step forward. "Everyone is just drunk." She stumbled on her feet and giggled. "I think I might also be drunk."

"I'm so embarrassed."

"Don't be. No one will remember," she assured her, her words slurring.

"Hopefully. I think I'm going to head back to the apartment now." Vanessa wanted to get away as quickly as possible before more tears fell.

"Let me come with you."

Vanessa wanted to tell her she could handle it herself, but the truth was she couldn't. Walking alone in the dark didn't make her feel very safe. She gave Erica a weak nod and the two of them began the short walk back to the apartment building.

When they reached the apartment building and got on the elevator, Vanessa took in a deep breath and gave Erica a nod.

"I'm sorry I ruined your night."

"You didn't," Erica assured her. "They usually aren't like that. I'm sorry."

"You don't need to apologize for them."

Vanessa rode up the extra level to Erica's apartment to make sure she made it inside safely. Then she went back to her apartment, glad the night was over. More tears spilled from her eyes.

I made it home, Vanessa typed to Bradley.

Did you have fun? You weren't out very late.

Vanessa chewed on the inside of her cheek. She debated telling Bradley the truth, but decided against it. Things seemed to be going great for Bradley and Vanessa wasn't about to change that because she had a bad evening.

Yes. Loads of fun. Just tired. Stayed up too late the night before.

Oh good! Can't wait to hear all about it.

Vanessa plugged her phone into its charging cable before sinking down onto her bed. She kicked off her shoes and glanced up at the fan above her. When she tried to close her eyes, she saw images that made her breath catch in her throat. She sat up sharply before swinging her legs over the side of the bed and standing.

The company sent over a basket when she first got her new job that had cheeses, cookies, and a large bottle of whiskey. Because of her promise to both her sister and herself, she'd hidden the whiskey far back in her closet, unable to just throw it away.

She entered her small closet and fell to her knees in search of the drink. Her hands dug through clothes until she felt the cold glass. Her eyes lit up. She pulled it out and stood, going straight to her kitchen for a glass. Once it was poured, she held it at her lips. For several seconds, she questioned if she was doing the right thing.

"*Shh…*" a voice whispered in her head. Her back shuddered and she took a sip.

Chapter Seventeen

V anessa reminded herself to play it cool while she was back at home. She prepped herself for what was to come, taking a deep breath. As she made her way through the airport, she saw her sister standing right outside of the security area. Before being seen, she placed a fixed smile on her face. Bradley spotted her then, smiling back and waving. The moment she stepped over the no pass line, her sister wrapped her arms around her neck and held her close. Vanessa hugged her back. She hadn't expected to feel such a rush of emotion being back home and with her sister.

"I'm so glad you're home!" Bradley exclaimed.

"Me too," Vanessa murmured, holding her tightly. "I'm glad to be back." They pulled away from one another, but Vanessa kept her hand on her arm. She hadn't realized until this moment how much she'd missed her sister.

"So, are you excited about your date?" Vanessa teased. She finally let go of her sister's arm as they made their way over to the baggage claim.

"Yes and no," Bradley answered.

"What do you mean by yes and no?"

"Oh, I don't know. Mom keeps asking me all these questions, and I'm worried she'll scare him away." Vanessa thought about all the phone calls she'd avoided from her, knowing her mother would ambush her when she saw her. Perhaps the excitement of Jones and Bradley would take some of the pressure off her.

"What kind of questions?"

They made it to the baggage claim just as the sound went off alerting everyone the bags would soon begin circling the belt.

"Um, if we're dating, if we're serious, if we've talked about having children," Bradley answered, her nose wrinkling up. "Mind you, all these questions were asked after I told her this would be our first time going out together and that it wasn't a real date."

"Ew," Vanessa said.

"Exactly. What color is your bag?"

"Yellow."

"Yellow?"

"Yes, I got it in New York, figured it would be easier to spot. Sorry about all the questions from Mom. She's ready to marry you off, you know? I've disappointed her by not being married and having a baby."

Bradley shook her head.

"No you haven't."

Vanessa scoffed.

"Oh, I have." She grabbed her suitcase, spotting it easily. It was heavy, but she managed to get it to the floor.

"What did you pack? You're only here for a few days."

"Yeah, well, I didn't know what all I would need." She pulled up the handle so she could drag the case behind her.

"So, tell me about New York. Have you made any friends?"

"Um, there's a co-worker named Erica who is pretty nice. We've hung out a few times. And New York is, New York. Not much to say about it."

Bradley's car was parked in the car garage across the street. Even with the wheels, Vanessa began to grow tired of pulling her heavy case. She was so glad when they finally reached her sister's car and she could throw it into the trunk.

"Your car has so much stuff in it," Vanessa commented. She shoved a few items out of the way so her carry-on could fit.

"I didn't expect you to bring this much. Now come on, Mom and Dad will be waiting for us at the restaurant."

"What?"

"Oh, surprise, we're going out to lunch."

Vanessa paused, her hand lingering on the door handle.

"I thought Dad had to work and Mom had Bingo today. I wasn't supposed to see them until later today when they got home."

"Oh, they've missed you. They wanted to come to the airport with me, but we all decided a surprise lunch would be more fun."

Vanessa let out a strangled laugh.

"Right, of course."

After Vanessa moved some papers off her sister's seat and sat down, she rested her head back against the headrest. Her fingers tapped against the side of the seat. She thought she had hours before seeing her parents, where she was planning to say she was tired and go to bed before too many questions were asked. Now it would be tough to avoid them all.

"You're quiet," Bradley said, driving out and onto the highway.

"Just tired." Vanessa turned her head to look at her sister. "I had to be at the airport early."

They continued to ride in silence before pulling up into the parking lot of a small, neighborhood restaurant that Vanessa hadn't been to in years. Her mouth watered thinking of their Monte Cristo sandwiches.

"Mom thought you'd want to eat here."

"I do like their food," Vanessa said. She got out of the car and glanced at the restaurant, with its faded sign and line out the front door of people waiting to get inside. "It's going to take hours to get a seat."

"Mom called and made a reservation."

"But it says in big letters they don't do reservations."

"Yeah, but Mom." Bradley shrugged.

"That poor person who had to talk with her on the phone."

They walked up to the restaurant, finding that their parents already had a table.

"Tell us everything about New York," her mother said excitedly, a bright smile on her face. "Oh, I just know it's been so exciting!"

"It's big," Vanessa simply replied. "Restaurants are open late. I like the food."

"And your job?"

"It's fine," Vanessa said. "It's a lot like my job was here, only a little different. I am in charge of more."

"And do you like it?"

Vanessa nodded, keeping her head down and focused on the dry skin on her thumb.

"Sure. It's great, really."

"Have you met anyone?" her mother then asked.

"Yes," Vanessa said, looking up. Her mother held a hopeful expression on her features. "I've made some friends." Her mother's face fell.

"What about a man?"

"No."

"Oh."

"You know," Vanessa began. "I think I'm taking dating off the menu for a while."

"Good idea," her father said, smiling. Her mother, however, was frowning in disappointment.

"But who knows what the future may bring," she quickly added. She'd told herself she was going to keep everyone happy this weekend and not show an ounce of her struggles.

"Yes, who knows," Bradley agreed. Their mother's face lit up.

"That's right! Who knows?"

Bradley entered Lucky Ones about half an hour before her shift. She walked behind the bar and grabbed her apron, tying it around her waist.

"Why are you here so early?" Jones asked.

"Vanessa was tired. She woke up early for her flight back and kept yawning. We all insisted she go on to bed. After she went to bed, I didn't want to sit there twiddling my fingers."

"Ah," Jones said.

Bradley twisted so she was now facing her employer. His eyebrow was raised, making the skin beside his eyes wrinkle, and there was a small smirk on his lips.

"Yeah," Bradley said. She felt tightness in her chest as her eyes couldn't remove themselves from Jones's mouth. He cleared his throat, causing her to jump slightly and advert her eyes back to his own. "Too much time with my parents can be a bad thing."

"I doubt that."

"Just wait until tomorrow night," Bradley told him. "You'll feel differently then." Her eyes shined, elated with what was to come. Even with her parents being there, she doubted anything could ruin it.

"I guess we'll see."

The door opened, dinging a bell, which made Bradley return her attention to cleaning the bar.

"It'll be a busy night," Jones said, glancing up at the clock. "Hope you're ready."

The dress Vanessa brought for the evening ended up being a little big around her chest. She hadn't put the dress on in over a year, and was surprised to see it didn't fit her like it used to. Vanessa stared at the lavender dress and tugged on it to make it sit correctly. She used some safety pins to pin it in place and then threw a thin white cardigan over her shoulders to hide the pins.

"Why are you wearing that cardigan?" her mother asked, walking into the room. She attempted to pull the cardigan from Vanessa's shoulders, but Vanessa shook her head and held it tightly at the front.

"It'll be cold inside."

"But the wedding itself is outside. Carry it with you, but don't hide your beautiful figure beneath that large cardigan."

"Mom, I'm not going to meet the love of my life tonight. I think this will be just fine."

Her mother grunted, preparing to say something else in regards to her outfit. However, instead of speaking more, she let the air out slowly and patted Vanessa's shoulders.

"Whatever you want, dear."

"Thank you." Vanessa turned one of her fresh curls with her fingers, fixing the way it had turned out away from her face. She dreaded what came after this weekend. Instead of focusing on that, she faced her mother. "You look beautiful."

Her mother wore a navy dress that flowed from the hips down. It was simple, but elegant.

"Oh, this old thing."

"You're being modest. You look amazing."

"Thank you. Your sister and Jones should be here shortly. Let's go out front and wait for them."

Jones brought her flowers. Even with his salt and pepper hair, he looked like a shy teenager when he handed them to her. Bradley brought the yellow roses up to her nose to smell them.

"These are nice," Bradley said.

"I just saw them when I was at the store earlier and thought why not." He let out a nervous chuckle.

Bradley went in search of something to put the flowers in. When she finally found a cup tall enough, she filled it with water and added the roses. She placed the cup in the middle of her small table. As she finished, she still saw Jones standing awkwardly in the doorway. He had his fingers looped in his belt buckle straps and he hummed beneath his breath. She smiled.

"Are you sure you're all right with picking up my parents and sister on the way to the wedding?"

"Of course."

"It's just we were told it has limited parking, and so it would be best if we all rode together," she explained. It wasn't the way she had envisioned tonight to go, but her father, especially, insisted they all ride together.

"I don't mind at all."

"Well, you say that now, until we're all crammed into your car with my parents," she said with a small laugh. "Sorry it has to be your car."

"As I said, I don't mind."

None of them had a car that comfortably fit five people in it. Yet, her parents still insisted they all fit into Jones's car, because his was the largest and did have five spots and five seatbelts. Vanessa was squished between her parents in the back, jealous of her sister who got to sit up front.

Her father liked to sit with his legs wide, giving her very little space for her own. Her mother didn't take up as much room, but she did keep leaning forward and squishing Vanessa in the process as she tried to talk more to Jones in the front seat.

"Tell me more about your family," her mother asked him.

Vanessa tried to maneuver her bottom to give herself some more space, but all it did was make the space between her and her parents tighter somehow. She sucked in a deep breath.

"I have a dad and a brother," Jones answered.

"Oh? And where do they live?"

Vanessa checked the time on the GPS up front. They still had thirty minutes until they arrived. She was growing hot in her sweater.

"There is supposed to be valet parking," her father said. "Make sure we take advantage of that! We brought a nice gift."

Finally they arrived at the venue and pulled up at the front. There were several people dressed in nice suits ready to take the cars and park them. Vanessa was so glad when she finally stepped outside and into the fresh air. She was already dreading the ride back home.

Jones held his arm out for Bradley to take it and Vanessa smiled. She wanted her sister to have a good evening.

CHAPTER EIGHTEEN

T he wedding had been lovely, but long. By the time they were heading to the reception, Vanessa's stomach was growling.

The venue for the reception was just across from where the wedding had been. It was a large conference hall that had been decorated with the wedding colors: gold and navy. The tables took up most of the area and there was a small dance floor over in the front, near the wedding cake. Vanessa looked for other food, but there was none. She remembered now it was a sit and wait to be served type of reception. Again, her stomach growled.

Up at the front was a woman who asked their names. When they gave it to her, she gave them their number for their own table. Theirs was up front and Vanessa saw there were some rolls sitting out for them. She couldn't wait to sit and grab one, but she had to find her name first.

As she walked around to each name plate and found hers, Vanessa also noticed the name beside hers: *Mr. Grey Walker.*

"Is this some joke?" Vanessa asked. She lifted up the name plate, her body growing warm from frustration and embarrassment. "I never RSVPed for two."

Bradley took the nameplate from her sister and studied it before she looked around the room.

"Maybe it's another guy with the same name?"

"How many Grey Walker's do you know?" Vanessa asked. Her palms grew sweaty. Grey couldn't be here tonight. She would not be able to keep up her façade if she came face to face with her ex-boyfriend, the guy she still considered to be the love of her life.

"Calm down, dear," her mother said in her patronizing tone. "We don't want to make a scene. I'm sure it's just some coincidence. Now, let's sit down, everyone else is and we're the only ones standing."

Bradley sat the nameplate back down, patting Vanessa's shoulders supportively, and then went to sit down next to Jones. Vanessa remained standing, her heart racing in her chest. Her mother tugged her hand.

"Sit," she commanded. Vanessa slid into her seat, continually glancing around the venue to see if she could spot Grey. Her mind tried to go through scenarios of what she'd do if he did show up here. Could she lie and say she wasn't feeling well? No, that would be too obvious. Maybe she could pretend she needed to help the bride with something, but what?

"You're just labeled as Jones," Bradley teased Jones.

"Because that's who I am."

"Will you ever tell us your first name?" her father asked.

"My name is Jones," Jones answered simply.

Laughter filled the table, but Vanessa was still distracted by her concern that Grey may end up sitting next to her at this table. Then a thought hit her: *Would he bring Emma?* She tried to see the name plate next to Grey's, but before she could, she heard his voice.

"Nessa?" his voice cracked. He stood before them with Emma on his arm. "What…um," he glanced around the entire table. Vanessa saw the flicker of panic on his face before he spotted her parents. "Mr. and Mrs. Price, Bradley, nice to see you all!"

Her mother stood, walking over to give Grey a big hug.

"We didn't expect to see you here. How do you know the bride and groom?" her mother asked him.

Vanessa held her breath and then let it out slowly to steady her heart. This was fine. She could handle this. Exes could be friends with one another.

"The groom is a friend from college."

"Ah."

"And you?"

"The bride is a cousin," Vanessa answered. The room's temperature was rising. She pulled on the collar of her dress.

"How strange we're all sat together," Emma said.

"Very strange," Vanessa agreed.

"It's a nice coincidence," Grey added. Both women frowned at his words before glancing uncomfortably at one another. "Let's sit."

It was awkward. The moment they sat, Grey was between his former love and his newest one. Vanessa grabbed one of the rolls and began to butter it. She needed to find something to do with her hands.

"How's the city?" Grey asked her. His hand remained intertwined with Emma's on the table between the two of them. Her fingers twiddled with each of his. Vanessa found it hard to draw her eyes away.

"It's a big city," Vanessa answered simply. She began to eat the roll, not caring that she was the only one eating.

"Do you like it?' he asked, his eyes baring into her.

"Sure, what's not to like."

"Oh! I love New York!" Emma gushed. "Grey and I have been talking about taking a trip up there soon. Maybe we could meet up."

"Um, maybe," Vanessa said. Her eyes widened when Emma's other hand came up to Grey's hand and she saw a flash of something shiny. As Emma's hand stopped moving, Vanessa saw the ring that Vanessa knew all too well. It was Grey's grandmother's ring, a ring which had been passed down to him after her death; a ring Grey always said he would give to her when he asked her to marry him. "You're–you're engaged?" The words escaped her mouth in a strained whisper.

Emma's hand rested on Grey's upper arm, making the light reflect off the diamond in the middle. She tilted her head toward Grey and brightly smiled.

"Yes," she said. "Grey proposed last month!" She held the brightness and excitement of a newly engaged woman. Even having her fiancé's ex in front of her did not deter her happiness.

"How wonderful," her mother said with forced excitement.

"Yes," Vanessa agreed. "Congratulations." A knot formed in the base of her throat as she felt the tears starting to build up behind her eyes. She knew she couldn't allow herself to give her sadness away, but as she tried to swallow down the tears it only grew worse.

"Congrats, Grey!" Bradley swooped in, coming over to give him a big hug and block both his and Emma's view from Vanessa. "How exciting! Ness and I have to go and say hello to our cousin, Mom's insisting. We'll be right back." Just like that, Bradley brought her arm below Vanessa's and lifted her out of the chair before walking her over toward their cousin, Maggie.

Vanessa glanced up, refusing to cry. She had no right to be upset that Grey was getting married. She should be happy for him; she did want him to be happy. She hiccupped.

Bradley curved to the right before they could approach their cousin and pulled them both into a small, empty corner of the venue. There was a bench by a window where Bradley insisted they both sit.

"Just take a moment to process it," Bradley said, rubbing soothing circles over Vanessa's back.

"I'm fine," Vanessa whispered. She didn't know who she was trying to convince: her or Bradley.

"I can't believe he's engaged already. You two broke up, what—less than a year ago? And he was so in love with you."

"Bradley, don't," Vanessa said with a heavy sigh.

"Maybe we could order you an Uber, or I could see if Jones would mind taking you back to the house, or—or I could say I'm feeling sick and we all could leave."

"No."

"Ness—"

"He'll know I'm leaving because I found out he's engaged. I'm not running away. I can handle this. I just need a moment, is all." Vanessa closed her eyes. She could do this. She could be happy for Grey and the rest of the evening would go smoothly.

"All right. We can take as long as you need."

"That was supposed to be my ring," Vanessa murmured. "And I screwed everything up."

"Vanessa, it isn't your fault. I still say if you tell Grey what you told me then he would—"

"It doesn't matter now, Bradley. He's moved on."

"I know, and I'm not saying you tell him to try to win him back. I say you tell him for closure, for yourself and him."

Vanessa leaned forward, running her hand over her face.

"I'm going to go walk around for a bit," Vanessa said in response. She stood, unable to talk in circles with her sister about this anymore. It no longer mattered. This had to be her closure.

Before her sister could say anything else, Vanessa walked into a crowd of people. The benefit of it being a large wedding was that Vanessa could disappear easily. Maybe a nice walk around the venue would make it easier for her to go back to her table in time for the cutting of the cake.

When Bradley made it back to the table, she saw both Grey and Emma were gone. Her parents were speaking with Jones, and she quickened her steps. She needed to know what they were talking about. She sat between her father and Jones, glancing between the three of them.

"So, what are you talking about?"

"Not much," her mother answered. "Where's Vanessa? I hope the engagement announcement didn't completely ruin her evening."

"She's a little shaken up, but she will be okay. This reception is boring, isn't it? What's the dance floor for if they're never going to play music?"

"Maybe I should go and look for your sister," her mother said, starting to stand up. Bradley's eyes widened and she shook her head.

"I'm sure she'll be fine, Mrs. Price. Why don't you let me go grab us all a drink from the bar?" Jones suggested.

Bradley looked at Jones with appreciation, because her mother sat back down and smiled.

"Sure," her mother said. "I'll take a sparkling water."

"And you both?"

"Wine," Bradley answered.

"A beer," her dad said.

Jones got up from his chair and his hand brushed along her back, making her grin up at him. He winked before disappearing off into the long line for drinks. Bradley watched him walking away, already ready for him to be back. They hadn't had much time to chat with one another alone, but she was still enjoying every moment with him.

"He's nice," her mother commented. "I like this Jones."

"You like him?" Bradley asked, surprised.

"Yes, why wouldn't I?"

"He's a bartender."

"So are you," her mother said.

"And he has tattoos."

"So do you," her mother said, her eyes glaring at the dragon tattoo on her shoulder.

"And you don't like either of those parts of me."

Her mother shrugged her shoulders. "It's different for a man."

There it was, Bradley thought. Her mother and her always different standards.

"Are you two dating?" her father asked.

"No, not yet or, well, I don't know," Bradley said, biting down on the inside of her cheek. "No," she finally settled on.

"But you want to?" He narrowed his eyes.

"Maybe—just, don't." Bradley felt the embarrassment rise up her cheeks.

"All right, we'll stop teasing you. Won't we?" her father asked her mother.

"Yes, dear."

As her parents thankfully changed their conversation, she noticed a wallet on the floor next to Jones's seat. Bradley bent down and grabbed it, opening it up to see who it belonged to. That's when she saw Jones's driver's license with his full name. She giggled.

"What? What are you laughing about?" She turned to find Jones standing behind her juggling several drinks in his hands.

"Not much, *Teddy*," she said, lifting his wallet up toward his face.

"Ted," he corrected.

"Oh Theodore, that's a distinguished name. You should be proud of such a name," her mother told him with a bright smile.

"It's just Ted. Not Theodore." He placed the drinks down and grabbed the wallet from Bradley's hands, placing it back into his pocket. Then he sat down next to Bradley and rolled his eyes. "Pretty proud of yourself, aren't you?"

"Yes, *Teddy*, very proud." She wiggled her brows and leaned toward him.

"Ted," he corrected, again. "Just Ted."

Bradley looked him up and down. She laughed again, giddy that she'd finally solved this riddle.

"You really don't look like what I imagine a Ted to look like."

"That's why I go by Jones. I hate my name." He wore a scowl on his face.

"Ted's not a bad name," Bradley said.

"So you'll stop teasing me about it?"

"Not likely. At least, not for a while."

Vanessa found a crowd between herself and her family's table. It had finally been announced that food would be arriving to the tables soon, and she was still starving. She felt a bit better now that she'd removed herself from everyone. She'd been able to gather up the courage to make it through the rest of the evening. It was only a few hours. She could handle a few hours.

"Excuse me. Excuse me," she said as she found her way between people. She bumped into someone and cursed beneath her breath.

"Oh, Vanessa! Are you having fun?" Emma placed her hand on Vanessa's. Vanessa's eyes fell to the ring that stared back up at her.

"Yeah," Vanessa said. She glanced back up to see Grey standing beside Emma. "Are you both?" She forced herself to smile.

"Not really," Grey said. "Where's the music? We've been walking around hoping to find someone we know."

"Well, now you've found me," Vanessa replied a bit too brightly. "They're supposed to be serving food soon."

"Finally!" Emma said. "I'm starved. I haven't eaten since noon. I should have brought a snack to sneak into the service."

Vanessa gave an anxious chuckle.

"Me too."

They turned to head back to their table when Vanessa came eye to eye with someone else. Her throat went dry and she tried to take a step back.

"Speak of the devil! Liam!" Grey said, moving up to give his friend a firm handshake. "I thought you were supposed to be here! How've you been?"

"Good, good," Liam said. He turned his gaze to Vanessa, making her chest tighten. "Vanessa, good to see you."

"Liam," she forced out.

"Glad to see you two are still together!" he said, but his blue eyes did not look away from her—the blue eyes that still haunted her every moment she shut her eyes. She felt trapped, like a bird in a cage.

"We're not," Vanessa said through clinched teeth. His eyes darkened and his lips curled up into a smirk.

"Meet my fiancée, Emma." Grey's words finally drew Liam's eyes away from her. He brought Emma closer to him.

"Fiancée? Wow, congrats, man."

"Thanks."

"When did you two meet?"

Vanessa decided to sneak away now that the conversation had moved away from her. She tried to turn, but a hand wrapped around her upper arm and pulled her back.

"Don't leave!" Emma said. "We're about to go and eat."

"Oh, where are you sitting? Maybe I could fit in at your table. I'm here all alone." His eyes were back on her.

"I…" Vanessa stuttered. "I…"

"Ness?" Grey's voice was full of concern. His hand touched her shoulder, causing her to jump. "Nessa, are you all right?"

"Um, yeah," she lied. "I need to go and…" She turned and made her way through the crowd, her heart racing. She heard steps coming up behind her and she panicked, hurrying her pace.

"Vanessa!" A hand grabbed her arm and she let out a blood curdling scream.

"Don't touch me!" Her face paled when she saw it was Grey.

"Nessa—what's wrong? What's happened?"

She inhaled sharply, very aware that everyone around them had grown quiet and was looking at her.

"Vanessa? Dear?" She turned her head to see her mother standing with the same worried expression Grey held.

Vanessa didn't know how to get herself out of the mess she'd gotten herself into. Everyone was still looking at her. She could feel the walls closing in. She began to run toward the only door she saw, hearing both of her parents calling after her.

"We should follow her," her mother said with true concern.

"No," Bradley stated. "No. Um, I'll go."

"I think we should all just give her some space," her father suggested.

"Right, right," Bradley agreed. She had no idea what had caused her sister's outburst. She struggled to believe Grey's engagement would have her screaming like that, but nothing else made sense. She rubbed her temple with the tips of her fingers.

"Are you all right?" Jones whispered to her. Her shoulders tensed.

"Yes. I kind of want to check on Vanessa, but maybe my dad is right. Maybe she needs space." Bradley rubbed her arms. Even though the building was packed with people, it was cold.

"Are you cold?"

"Yes."

"Let me go and grab you a jacket from the car."

"You don't have to do that."

"I don't mind." Jones stood from the table, giving her a small smile. "Do you need anything else?"

"No."

As he walked away, Bradley felt warmness spread over her. None of the other men she'd dated ever cared this much after her, making sure she was completely taken care of.

"He's a catch," her mother whispered in her ear. "If you don't claim him, I might ditch your father and date him myself."

"Oh, Mom, don't." Bradley gagged. "*Don't* say such a thing."

"Why not? Am I not allowed to find men attractive?"

"Not the ones that I do!"

Jones exited the building, glad to be out of the noise and crowd. As more of an introvert, he was glad for a moment outside to collect himself.

Turning the corner, he spotted Vanessa sitting on a bench, turned away from him with her shoulders shaking every few seconds. He frowned. He stood there for a moment wondering if he should say something to her or walk away quietly. The last thing he wanted to do was upset her more. When a louder sob left her lips, he couldn't help but speak up.

"Vanessa?"

She turned quickly, wiping under her eyes and glancing up at him. Her lower lip quivered as she tucked her head back down.

"I…I'm sorry," she whispered.

"There's absolutely no reason to apologize to me," Jones said, taking a seat down next to her. His words didn't appear to reach the woman before him. Her body shook as she tightened her hands over her knees, causing the skin around her fingers to turn pink from the pressure.

"I was really trying," she murmured as her eyes wandered over toward the empty bench across from them. "But I can't—I don't know who I am anymore."

"You don't have to know who you are," Jones said. "Throughout life, that changes. It's part of the journey."

"No!" Vanessa cried. "You don't understand. I am supposed to know." She hit her hand against her chest emphatically. "I'm Vanessa. I'm the good child. I'm the one who has her shit together. I'm the one who did everything right. All of my life, I've never stepped out of line. And lately, I just can't seem to get myself together. I tried, I did. But—"

"I don't know about that, Vanessa. You've got a great job in New York. You—"

"I quit my job," Vanessa confessed, her voice low. She let out an uneasy chuckle.

"Oh," Jones murmured.

She curled forward, hugging her body tightly. Jones wished he knew the right things to say to Vanessa to bring her comfort. He didn't know what happened to take her down this path she was on right now, but he did wish he had the tools to fix it all for her.

"I haven't told my family or Bradley, yet. I go back to New York in two days to finish up my two weeks, and then I have nothing. Nowhere to live, no place to go. I don't even know why I quit. I just didn't want to do it anymore. My parents are going to be so disappointed." Vanessa untucked her arms from around her before pressing her palms against her eyes.

Jones glanced around, but he was the only one here. His hand came up to her shoulder and he just sat with her for a moment, not saying anything as Vanessa sobbed.

"I'm sure there was a good reason for you to quit, even if it just was because you didn't want to do it anymore," Jones whispered a moment later.

"I'm sorry. I shouldn't have pulled you into any of this," she whispered, placing her hands by her sides and glancing up at him. Her eyes held so much pain within them—pain that Jones felt this immense need to ease away. "Why don't you go back inside? My ride should be here soon."

"Ride?"

"I called an Uber. I think it's best if I leave and not draw any more attention away from the bride and groom."

"I'll wait here with you, until the Uber arrives."

Vanessa's eyes searched his face and her lower lip quivered. Jones's hand came up to brush a stray hair that had fallen over her cheek. Their eyes met for a brief moment before Vanessa ducked her head away.

On the ride back from the wedding, Jones kept thinking back to sitting on the bench outside the wedding with Vanessa. She'd been distraught; beyond anything he could do to help her. So he'd just sat until the car arrived to pick her up. He'd found he hadn't been too keen on the idea of letting the distraught Vanessa get into a car with a driver he didn't know, and he couldn't put his finger on why it unnerved him so much.

He shook it off as being overprotective of both her and Bradley. Bradley had been drugged in his bar. It was only natural for him to worry about them both. Especially Vanessa when she was so upset.

"I can't believe Grey's engagement upset her that much," Bradley's mother was saying in the backseat.

"It did surprise me," Bradley agreed. She turned to him and he gave her a quick glance. Bradley's eyes were staring at him for more answers, but as he'd told her before he knew just as much as she did.

Again, Vanessa's face filled his thoughts. Why did he wish he'd gone with her?

They dropped Bradley's parents off at their house before Jones drove Bradley home. She grinned when he opened the door for her, stepping out onto the cement. He held his hand out to her and she took it. There was a bounce in her step. Jones wasn't naive to the fact that Bradley liked him. And he had to admit, he enjoyed spending time with her too.

When they reached her door, Bradley placed her key into the lock. She turned it and partially opened the door before looking back at him. This was his moment. He bent over slightly, watching as Bradley's breath hitched in her throat. Their noses touched, and he paused. *This isn't right*, he thought. He pulled back, leaving Bradley's mouth partially open and waiting.

"Goodnight, Bradley," Jones said. She gawked before fixing her face.

"Goodnight, Jones."

He stood there for a brief moment, wondering if there wasn't something he should say. Instead he gave a quick nod and walked away.

Bradley remained at her doorway, thinking about what just happened. He'd nearly kissed her. They'd been so close. So why did he stop right then? Before she could think any more about it, she heard a sob. Her ears perked up, wondering if it was one of her neighbors. But as the sound reoccurred, she realized the sound was coming from inside her apartment. Bradley pushed open her door to find her sister sitting in her bed, hunched over, and crying.

"Vanessa?" At the sound of her name, her sister looked up. Vanessa used the flat of her palms to wipe away the tears, but they kept coming.

"I–I'm sorry. I didn't …I couldn't go back to our parents' house. I…"

Bradley rushed to her sister's side.

"I'm sorry he's getting married, Ness. I'm sorry you had to see him tonight," she murmured, rubbing her sister's back with wide circles.

"He…he was there," Vanessa said between heavy breaths.

"I know," Bradley soothed. "I know."

"No, him. *Him*," Vanessa said strongly, hitting her chest with her hand. Bradley's eyes grew.

"Him?" The realization hit Bradley and she blanched. "Do you mean Liam?"

At the sound of the man's name, Vanessa sucked in a harsh breath.

"Oh my god."

"I…Bradley, I said no," Vanessa sobbed. "I said no!"

Chapter Nineteen

10 Months Ago

Vanessa carefully ran the lipstick over her lips, judging whether this particular shade of red suited her. She frowned, grabbing a tissue to wipe it away.

"Don't!" Grey called out. "I like that color."

Vanessa grinned, turning to face him. "Really? Bradley got it for me. She said I needed more pops of color in my life."

"Ah. Well, it looks nice on you, but if you don't like it, don't wear it."

"No, I will," Vanessa said. She brought her arms up to rest on his shoulders, drawing him closer to her. "As long as you don't think it's too much."

"I don't." Grey bent forward to kiss her. Vanessa melted into his lips and moaned in content.

"So what's your old college friend's name?" Vanessa asked, reluctantly pulling away from his lips. She brought her hand to the back of his head to play with the hairs at the nape of his neck.

"Liam Moore," he said before kissing right below her ear, causing wonderful shivers to spread down her spine. He lifted his head and their foreheads touched.

"Right, Liam. Are you sure you want me to come along tonight? Wouldn't you prefer to catch up with him on your own?" She continued to run her fingers through his hair.

"Of course not, we've both been so busy with work lately. I want to spend whatever time with you I can."

They went downtown for dinner to one of their favorite tapas restaurants. It was underground with dark mood lighting and live music. Grey opened the door for her and let her in before coming up behind her to place his hand on her lower back. He then waved.

"He's right back there."

They headed straight back to the table where Liam sat. Grey introduced them both and then they sat down. Liam had already ordered their first course. For nearly an hour they spoke as though they'd known one another for a decade. Liam was a charming man. He had these piercing blue eyes that lit up every time he laughed.

"Have you told Vanessa about the time you got arrested?" Liam asked.

"No, he hasn't," Vanessa said, facing Grey and narrowing her eyes. "*You* got arrested?"

"Liam!" Grey stammered with an uneasy laugh. "You're going to get me in trouble."

"So were you?" Vanessa asked again, playfully.

"Yes," Grey answered, tugging on his collar. "But it wasn't like what you're thinking. It was just some frat party nonsense. I wasn't even charged." He placed his hand over Vanessa's. "Though, I did get lucky. I was being an idiot."

"Aren't we all when we're young?" Liam mused.

"I wasn't," Vanessa said smugly.

"It's true." Grey gave Vanessa a wink. "Vanessa here puts us all to shame."

"Surely you have some skeletons in the closet," Liam said. He moved forward, taking Vanessa in with his eyes.

"No," Vanessa replied. At the same time, Grey said,

"Her only little secret is a small tattoo."

"Grey!" Vanessa shot him a look.

"Where is it?" She grew uncomfortable when Liam eyed her over.

"That's a secret you don't get to know," Grey said with a gleam in his eye. His phone began ringing. He glanced at the screen before jumping up from the table and going to a quiet corner to talk.

"You're dating a good guy there." Vanessa nodded at Liam.

"He's the best," she said. "I don't know what I would do without him."

Grey came right back over, but he didn't sit down.

"That was my assistant. All of the grades I turned in for midterms got deleted. He can't seem to figure out how to fix it. I have to go in and fix it before the morning. I'm going to be up all night; I'll probably have to sleep on the couch in my office. I'm sorry, Liam. I need to take Vanessa home. Can we reschedule?"

"Oh, we just ordered our dessert," Liam said. "Couldn't you stay for that?"

"I'll pay. You stay and eat," Grey told Liam. "Come on, darling. Sorry we have to leave so soon."

Vanessa began to get up, but Liam placed his hand over hers. She glanced at him as he looked up at Grey.

"Why don't you let Vanessa stay and eat too? No need for her to leave and miss out on her dessert. I can drive Vanessa back."

"What do you think?" Grey asked Vanessa. She chewed on the inside of her cheek, but nodded. It seemed innocent enough. Plus, she had been excited about her chocolate cake.

"Sure, I guess."

"Are you sure?" Grey questioned Liam. "You really don't mind?"

"Absolutely."

Grey kissed the top of Vanessa's head before giving Liam a hug and exiting the restaurant. Liam ordered them another round of drinks.

"I guess work keeps him busy," Liam said.

"Oh, always. We're both always busy. It's been hard for us to find time for one another lately," Vanessa told him. She took a big sip of her drink, trying to settle her nerves.

Everything after that became a blur. She could only recall a moment here or there, like giving Liam their address and a hand on her back, pushing her forward.

"Shh, now, he won't know a thing."

The world spun and she closed her eyes.

"What?" she breathed. She found she was laying down with a body hovered over her. "Grey?"

But it wasn't Grey's face. Blue, icy eyes stared down at her. She reached her hands out to push against his chest.

"No," she murmured, her eyesight growing hazy. "No."

The next morning, Vanessa awoke with no memories from the night before. She felt dazed, pressing the heel of her hand against her forehead. How much had she had to drink?

She heard the sound of footsteps near her doorway. She jerked up, making her head pound harder. Was Grey here? She thought she remembered him telling her he'd be staying in his office all night.

But as she turned her head, she saw Liam standing in her doorway, buttoning up his shirt, with his black boxer shorts poking beneath the fabric of his shirt. Vanessa pulled her sheet up over her bare chest.

"What-what are you doing here?" she gasped. "Where is Grey? *Why* are you in my house?"

A sinister smile grew on his lips as he came closer toward the bed.

"Oh, so that's how you're playing this? You insisted I come inside your house last night to have wine."

"What?" Vanessa shook her head. None of that sounded familiar. Liam stepped forward, pressing his knuckles against the bed and leaning closer to her.

"Don't worry," he whispered, "I won't tell Grey. It'll be our little secret."

"I didn't sleep with you!" Vanessa yelled. "I wouldn't!"

"Look, we had a lot to drink and had a bit of fun. That's all it was. No harm, no foul."

"No harm?! No foul?! No, no!" Vanessa stood, dragging the blanket from the bed with her to keep her figure covered.

"No need to hide, sweetheart, I saw all of you last night. I even got a peek at that nice little tattoo on your hip. Very sexy." He licked his lips.

"Get out!" Vanessa screamed, pointing toward her front door.

"Vanessa—"

"Get out!"

Bradley poured some milk into her coffee, yawning even though it was already ten. She had been out too late with her friends the night before. Bradley went to sit down but before she could, there came an anxious knock on her door.

Bradley walked over to the door and checked the peephole. When she looked through the hole and saw it was her sister, she swung open the door.

"Well, this is a surprise—" Bradley paused her words upon seeing her sister's face. Vanessa's eyes were puffy and red, and her shoulders shook from what appeared to be the aftershocks of crying. "Come in."

Vanessa stepped inside, pacing the small apartment.

"Nessa? What's going on? What's happened?"

"I...I cheated on Grey," Vanessa admitted. She stopped her steps, glancing up to meet Bradley's eyes. She sobbed. "Oh, what have I done?"

"Wait, what?" Bradley asked, not quite believing her. Vanessa loved and adored Grey. "No, that doesn't sound like you, Vanessa. Tell me *exactly* what happened."

"Grey and I went to dinner last night with his friend, Liam. He had to go into work last night, so Liam took me home. I can't remember most of the night. I guess I invited him in. He said we drank a lot." Vanessa rubbed her fingers against her temple.

"Wait a minute," Bradley said, the dots connecting in a way that made her stomach turn. "You said you can't remember most of the night? What do you remember? Do you remember inviting him in?"

"No."

"Do you remember drinking?"

"Um, a glass or two of wine at dinner." More sobs came. "What have I done? Grey will never forgive me!"

Bradley placed her hands on her sister's shoulders.

"You only had two glasses of wine?" Bradley asked.

"Yes, I mean, no—I must have had more, or I don't know."

"Shh," Bradley soothed. "You didn't do anything wrong, Ness. I don't think you slept with this Liam guy willingly." Bradley was cautious with her words, giving it a moment to sink in. The color on Vanessa's face drained.

"No," Vanessa whispered.

"It sounds like he drugged you, Nessa."

"No! That doesn't even make sense. Why would Liam...no." She shook her head. "You're just trying to make this better for me, because you're my sister, because I can never do anything wrong. But I did, Bradley! I screwed up! I slept with this Liam guy. I ruined everything!"

"Vanessa—"

Her sister drew her hands over her face, unwilling to listen.

CHAPTER TWENTY

She finally did it. Her sister finally admitted to herself what really happened that fateful night. Bradley stayed up with her, listening as she just kept saying the words "I said no," over and over again. Her sister repeated those words until finally falling into a fitful sleep. But Bradley couldn't sleep. All night, she kept her eyes on her sister, with her tear-tracked cheeks and runny nose.

When the sun rose, Bradley tiptoed out of the bed. She needed coffee, but she wanted to let Vanessa sleep as long as she could. She walked around the edge of the bed, cursing loudly as her knee hit the corner.

"Shit!" She covered her mouth, darting her eyes toward Vanessa. Vanessa stirred, moaning before turning back over to her side and covering her face with a pillow.

Bradley continued her short journey, grateful when she made it to the kitchen without any more mishaps. She opened the cabinet where she held the coffee grounds. The moment she grabbed the container, several more things fell out with it. She grimaced with each sound as the various items from her unorganized cabinet fell to the countertop.

"Wh–what?" Vanessa shot up from the bed, eyes wide.

"Sorry," Bradley apologized, giving a sheepish look. "I was trying to be quiet."

Vanessa rubbed her eyes and yawned.

"What time is it?"

"Six. It's early."

"Oh." Vanessa grew quiet, pulling her legs up to her chest. Bradley started the coffee and then made her way back over by her sister.

"Do you want to talk about it?" Bradley asked. Vanessa glanced up at the ceiling, blinking back tears. Her attempt to quell her tears didn't work, and before Bradley knew it, Vanessa had broken down yet again. Once more, Bradley wrapped her arm around her sister and brought her close. "Let it all out."

"It's not fair," Vanessa said between her tears. "He–he gets to move forward with his life, and I...I...I..."

"You could go to the police, tell them what happened," Bradley suggested.

"No," Vanessa answered sharply. "No. It's too late for any of that. They–they'll never believe me. I won't do it; I–I can't. I just want to forget it ever happened."

Bradley sighed. "You tried that before and it didn't quite work out the way you wanted it to."

Vanessa shot her a glance before sliding off the bed and grabbing her sweater from the chair beside her. She tugged it on, hugging her arms across her chest. Vanessa stood there for a moment, her lower lip twitching before her resolve faded and she broke down again. She hunched forward, hiding her face in her hands as her shoulders shook with each sob. Bradley exhaled, jumping up and standing next to her.

"You're going to have to face this, Ness," she murmured, rubbing her sister's back. "You can't ignore it any longer. You can't pretend it didn't happen. You can't try to make yourself the bad guy in an attempt to not have to face what really happened." Bradley paused a beat, trying to ease her sister into the next words. "You were raped."

Vanessa's sobs grew louder.

"I can't do this anymore," Vanessa cried. There was a finality to her words which made a shiver rise up Bradley's spine.

"Nessa—"

"Don't worry. I'm not going to do anything drastic," Vanessa said as she attempted to wipe her tears away. She started looking around Bradley's apartment, in search for her things. "I'm just—not sure what I'm going to do. I don't have a job anymore."

"You don't have a job?" Bradley asked, shocked. "What do you mean, you don't have a job?"

"I quit," Vanessa said, matter of fact. She grabbed her phone. "I'm going to see if I can change my flight for today."

Bradley snatched the phone from her sister, earning a growl from Vanessa.

"Give that back!"

"No! You need to sit down and just, sit for a minute. What do you mean you quit your job?"

Vanessa's nose flared. She tried to grab her phone back, but Bradley hid it behind her back and pointed to the bed. Defeated,

Vanessa sat. Bradley sat beside her, keeping the phone hidden from Vanessa's view.

"I couldn't do it anymore, Bradley. I couldn't pretend to be the old me with that job up in New York. It was…stifling. I–I don't know what to do," she murmured. "I don't even know who I am anymore, Bradley. And I'm always scared—terrified that I'll never figure it out."

Bradley brought her hand up to tuck Vanessa's hair behind her ear. She didn't know how to make this better for her sister. Vanessa had always been the one looking after her. She dropped her hand and rested her head on Vanessa's shoulder before taking her hand within her own.

"You don't have to figure it out right now, Ness. Right now, you only have to focus on coming to terms with what happened. It won't happen overnight. You won't ever forget it. But one day, you will feel more like yourself again. One day, you'll be happy."

"I hope that's true."

Hours later, Vanessa found herself sitting on a bench across from where Grey worked. She didn't quite know how she'd ended up here. After her and Bradley's talk, she left her sister's apartment saying she just needed some air. Then she winded up here; a place where she and Grey would sometimes sit together when they had a few minutes during their lunchtime to see one another.

She picked at the skin around her nails, glancing back up at the large building. Grey wasn't even working today. He was probably at home with Emma, planning their future together.

Someone sat beside her. She scooted away from the figure and turned away.

"I didn't think I'd make you feel uncomfortable," a familiar voice said. Vanessa looked back to see it was Jones. He was already standing.

"No, sit," she said. "What are you doing here?"

Jones lifted a small paper bag.

"Bagels. I come down here every Sunday for bagels from the bagel shop around the corner."

"Oh."

"And what are you doing here?"

"I'm not sure." Vanessa felt the tears coming again. She pressed her fingers against the edge of her eye. "I bet you're tired of finding me on a bench crying. You'd likely been better off just pretending you hadn't seen me."

Jones shook his head and sat back down beside her. It was nice to have him join her, so she didn't have to be alone. He reached into the paper bag, pulling out one of the bagels and offering her one. Vanessa took it. The bagel was warm to the touch. She brought it up and took a large bite.

"Wow," she said, her mouth watering and wanting for more.

"Yeah, they're good."

Vanessa devoured the bagel, not realizing just how hungry she'd been. Jones pulled another bagel out of the bag before offering it to her.

"No," Vanessa said. "Those are your special treat. I shouldn't be eating them all."

"I can always get more."

"I really don't need more." But she couldn't keep her eye off the bagel. Her tongue could already taste it. Jones placed it in her hand.

"You want it. Eat it."

Vanessa gave him a grateful smile. She did as he told her, but this time she took her time to enjoy each bite. Once she finished the second bagel, Jones handed her a napkin. She dabbed the napkin against each corner of her lips before balling up the napkin and holding it in her hand.

"My former boyfriend works in that building," Vanessa said, pointing to the building in front of them. "We planned on getting married, him and me. We wanted two kids, a boy and a girl." She chuckled at how ridiculously ordinary it all sounded.

"But now he's engaged to someone else?"

"Yes." Vanessa tucked her hands under her thighs and leaned forward. "I broke it off with him. I told him it wasn't what I wanted, not anymore. I broke his heart."

"Why? Was that how you really felt?"

"No. I loved him. I still love him." She knitted her brows and bit back the sobs that wanted to escape.

"Then why did you break up with him?"

Vanessa withdrew her hands from under her legs and turned to face Jones. His face was full of concern instead of curiosity, much like the way he'd looked at her the day before. Something about his expression made her know she could trust him.

"Because his friend raped me." The words stung her tongue and her breath hitched in her throat. It was the first time she'd said those words out loud. "I should go," she said. She couldn't believe she'd just admitted her deepest secret to him.

"Does he know?" Jones asked. His jaw clenched.

"No." She stood from the bench and grabbed her bag from the side. "Thanks for the bagels and sitting with me."

"You should tell him," Jones said, raising his brow.

"I–I don't know. It doesn't matter, not anymore."

"I disagree. If this man loved you like you said he did, then he needs to know the truth. He deserves to know it."

Vanessa met his gaze. Jones's eyes were intense, full of anger and passion. She swallowed hard.

"Goodbye, Jones. Thanks again."

She changed her flight to a few hours earlier than her original departure. Deciding not to tell her sister or anyone she was leaving early, she'd snuck out of her sister's apartment earlier that morning, just needing to get away. Once again, she was running away from her problems.

Right as she got into the security line, she spotted her sister running up to her and waving her down.

"Ness! Vanessa!"

"How–how did you know I was going to be here?" Vanessa asked.

"I checked upcoming flights when I woke up and you were gone."

Vanessa sighed. She walked toward her sister and further away from the security line.

"You could live with me," Bradley offered. "When you get back."

"You came all this way to tell me I can stay with you after I have nowhere to live? Who even said I was coming back to Georgia?"

"Are you not?" Bradley asked, placing her hands on her hips.

"I am."

"Well, there you go. You can stay with me. That'll give you time to figure this all out, Ness."

"The two of us in your small apartment? I think we'll hate each other by the end of the first week. I'll figure it out," Vanessa said.

"We could get a futon, put up a sheet like we did when we had to share a room those few months when Grandpa Eddie moved in."

That made Vanessa smile.

"I'm the big sister," she reminded Bradley. "I don't need you taking care of me. I'll probably just stay with Mom and Dad, if they'll have me. It'll be fine."

"Have you even spoken to Mom and Dad since the wedding? I'm guessing not, because they've been calling me every hour or so, and I am sure they're blowing up your phone."

"I don't know what to say to them. They're going to be so disappointed in me." She took in a deep breath. She'd turned off her phone last night, unable to take the never ending phone calls from her parents. She texted them an 'I'm sorry' and that she'd call them after she was back in New York before turning it off.

"They love you. Remember, I'm still the screw up." Bradley winked. "And you can stay with me. We'll make it work. You don't have to tell Mom and Dad what happened, but maybe you should tell them something. They love you."

"Hmm," Vanessa said, "that sounds similar to what Jones said about telling Grey."

"Jones?" Bradley asked, surprised. "What does Jones have to do about any of this?"

"I ran into him downtown yesterday, and I told him what happened to me. I don't even know why..." Vanessa's eyes glanced at the large clock on the wall which said she still had an hour to get to her gate.

"Because he made you feel safe," Bradley said, frowning.

"Or because he was there and he hardly knows me." Vanessa touched her sister's upper arm. "Thanks for being there for me. I'll be all right. I'll figure out how to tell our parents I don't have a job any more, and I'll stay with them. You deserve to have a life of your own without taking care of me." She readjusted her bag over her shoulder.

"I don't mind."

"I know and I love you for it."

In just the few minutes they'd been talking, the line for security had doubled.

"I need to go through security. I'll call you when I get to New York. Love you." She kissed her sister's cheek, and Bradley kissed her back.

"Love you, too."

Bradley still hadn't caught up from her lack of sleep the other night. She hadn't been able to rest during the day either; she was too worried about her sister.

Now at the end of her shift, she was struggling to keep her eyes open. Jones came around her, taking the rag from her hand.

"You should go on home. I can clean up for the evening."

Bradley yawned.

"Are you sure?"

"Yes. Though, can you drive? Maybe I should take you home," he said. "I can't have you getting in an accident."

"Are you sure?"

"Yes. Go sit down and I'll grab the keys for the car."

"You don't want to take me on the bike?" she teased.

"Not with you that tired." Jones disappeared in the back and Bradley sat down at the bar. She couldn't wait to be in her bed, asleep. She rubbed her eyes, trying to keep herself awake until she got home. Now that she knew her sister was safe in New York, maybe she could actually get a full eight hours of sleep.

While Jones was in the back getting his keys, Bradley thought back to what Vanessa had told her earlier. She'd told Jones about what happened to her. Why would she do that? Vanessa brushed it off as him being there in the moment and her hardly knowing him. But that wasn't true. Vanessa knew Jones pretty well, Bradley would say. Was there something she was missing? She thought about asking Jones about it, but what would she say?

Jones returned back to the bar, lifting his keys in his hand to show her.

"Ready to go?"

"Yes, please. Um, did you talk to Vanessa yesterday?" Bradley asked him. Jones nodded.

"Yeah, I saw her over by the bagel place. Why?"

Bradley stared at him a moment before shaking her head. "No reason. Let's go."

Jones drove her home and she nearly fell asleep on the way. When they reached her apartment, he opened the car door and then walked her up to her apartment.

Bradley stared at him, breaths heavy. Jones gave her a small smile, but he didn't attempt to lean toward her. Whatever Bradley thought she felt earlier between the two of them was no longer there. She wondered if she'd imagined it all.

"Thank you for bringing me home, Teddy," she teased, in an attempt to lighten her own mood. Jones chuckled and rolled his eyes.

"You're never going to let that go, are you?"

"Nope. I think it sort of suits you, you know? Teddy Jones, looks a bit rough on the outside, but is a sweet teddy bear on the inside."

Jones huffed.

"Goodnight. Take tomorrow off if you need it. I can have Casey cover."

"Okay." Bradley stepped into her apartment and closed the door behind her. She locked it and peeped through the peephole to see Jones still standing there. He scratched his chin and then sighed before walking away.

Chapter Twenty-One

Her last two weeks in New York were full of finishing up projects and lunches with Erica. Erica had become a good friend to her in the short time she'd lived here. It was hard to tell her goodbye. Of course, they both promised to keep in touch. Vanessa was sure they would, for a while, but over time their relationship would likely fade. Long distance friendships rarely held up, especially when they'd only known one another for a short time.

When she arrived in Savannah, she texted Erica, telling her she was back home.

Glad you made it safely!

She dropped her phone back into her bag and walked over to her sister who was waiting for her on the other side of security. This hug was shorter than last time.

"Thanks for picking me up again."

"You *are* my sister," Bradley said.

"I spoke with Mom and Dad when I got back to New York."

"Yes, I know. They told me. How'd it go?"

"I don't know. Mom had about a million questions; Dad kept asking if I was okay. I don't think they're very happy about any of it," Vanessa said, biting on her lower lip. "No, I know they weren't. Mom cried."

"Cried?"

"Yes, asked me what she did wrong."

Bradley rolled her eyes.

"Mom can be so dramatic. Don't let it get to you."

"Yeah," Vanessa said uneasily. She'd been avoiding talking to her parents since that phone call. It was just easier. "I don't have a job yet, but I do have a place."

"Oh?"

"I was able to use the money from the sale of the house to get an apartment," Vanessa explained. "My realtor helped me find it last minute. She's a godsend."

"Where is it?"

"Not too far from yours, I think. I have the address somewhere," Vanessa said, digging in her purse. She found the crumpled up piece of paper and shoved it into her sister's hand. "Do you mind taking me there?"

"Sure," Bradley answered.

They walked outside and to Bradley's car. It had less stuff in it this time and Vanessa had plenty of room for her bags.

The moment she sat down in her seat, her sister shoved a card into her hand.

"Here."

"What's this?"

"This is Addiso therapist. Addison always preaches about how she's the best. I've made you an appointment for next week."

"What?" Vanessa breathed with a shake of her head. "I don't need therapy, Bradley. I'm fine."

"You're not," Bradley disagreed.

"I am."

"Alright. Tell me, what is your plan for life?" Bradley looked at her pointedly.

"Not having a plan doesn't mean I'm not okay. You seem to do just fine bouncing around from job to job and having no big goals."

"Yes, but you are not me," Bradley said. "And I haven't been self-sabotaging myself."

Vanessa sighed. She turned the small card around to read the name on the front: Valeria Miles.

"What would I even say to her?"

"Whatever you want." Bradley turned on the car before turning back to look at Vanessa. "You know, there's nothing wrong about getting help. Someone took advantage of you. Violated you. I can't imagine how that messes with your head."

"Do you really think she could help with that?" Vanessa whispered, her sister's words feeling heavy on her chest.

"I should hope so."

Vanessa stared at the card for a long minute before saying, "Alright. I'll give her a try."

Vanessa stepped into her new apartment with her sister trailing behind her. She'd been able to do all the paperwork over the phone. Her realtor had set up her place with an air mattress, some food, and toiletries to hold her over until Vanessa could go shopping.

"Look at that, there's even a TV," Bradley said as she checked out Vanessa's place.

"Yeah, I ordered it and had it shipped to this address. The realtor must have set it up for me. She's honestly the best. I'm going to have to do something nice for her as a thank you."

"Well, I'm going to have to let you enjoy your space to yourself. I have to get to work, but call me later. Maybe we can do lunch tomorrow?" Bradley came over next to her and gave her a quick hug.

"Maybe."

"And call Mom and Dad. Let them know you're home safely," Bradley said as she left the apartment.

Now that Vanessa was alone, she opened her suitcase. Inside her checked bag were two bottles of whiskey she hadn't wanted her sister to see. Bradley would have made a bigger deal out of it than it was. She wouldn't understand how the liquid helped settle Vanessa's nerves and block out the memories that seemed to never leave her alone, ever since she'd remembered that night more clearly.

She placed the two bottles down next to the sink and checked the time. Her sister was right, she should call their parents. But before that, she needed a few sips of her drink to help her through the conversation. Deep down, she knew it was a dangerous game she was playing—using the alcohol more and more to make it through each day.

She took a few sips from her cup and she was ready to call her mom.

"Vanessa! How are you, dear?" Vanessa hadn't been expecting to hear her mother sound so cheerful.

"Fine," Vanessa croaked. She swallowed, and tried to sound brighter. "I made it to my new apartment. It's really nice."

"So you have an apartment?" Vanessa didn't miss the not-so-subtle disappointment in her mother's voice from not knowing what was going on with Vanessa's life, yet again.

"Um, yeah. I thought it would be best to have a place of my own."

"So you're back in Savannah, then?"

"Yes. I told you I'd be back today."

"That's right. It's just been so long since you've spoken to me or your dad, I'd forgotten."

Vanessa rubbed her temple.

"I don't know what you want me to say, Mom. But yes, I'm back."

The line remained silent for a moment, making Vanessa feel guilty. She could still remember her mother crying on the other end when she finally called her back after she made it to New York.

"Well," her mother started, breaking the silence. "Why don't we all have dinner in a few days after you've had time to settle into your new place? All of us; you, me, Dad, and Bradley. How does that sound?"

"Sure, sounds good," Vanessa lied. The last thing she wanted was to be eye to eye with her mother. It would be hard to escape her then.

Vanessa was glad that their conversation remained short. The moment she got off the call, she poured herself a second glass of whiskey. As she lifted it to her lips, she paused. Her hand withdrew the business card from her back pocket and she looked at it. On the corner, Bradley had marked the date and the time for her upcoming appointment. Vanessa sat the drink back down on the countertop.

"Alright," she whispered to herself, "you win." Vanessa walked it over to the refrigerator and used the one magnet she had to keep it up as a reminder not to miss it.

Chapter Twenty-Two

It took Vanessa hours to pick out the best outfit for dinner. She already knew tonight was going to be a disaster—with her parents telling her how disappointed they were in her life choices as of late—the last thing she needed on top of that was her mother saying something about her outfit.

Once she finally settled on what she was wearing, Vanessa curled her hair exactly how her mother preferred it and put on a layer of make-up. Without it, her mother would say she looked sickly; she couldn't have that, either.

She got a notification on her phone informing her that her taxi was nearby. Vanessa grabbed her purse and headed straight outside to keep her eyes out for the car that would be picking her up. Eventually, she'd need to get herself her own vehicle. She had to start over with every single thing. While for some people a new start might be exciting, it terrified her. Never in her life had she been so lost.

However, she wouldn't let that show to her parents or her sister. She was going to put on a brave face and act as though this all exactly how she wanted it to be.

The taxi arrived. She got in, bouncing her knees the entire ride to her parents' house. She was already regretting not having at least one glass of whiskey to get her through the evening.

When she arrived at the house, she stared out the window for a long while, terrified to get out of the car. It wasn't until the driver cleared his throat that she finally opened the door and stepped onto her parents' driveway.

The moment she started walking up, her parents' front door swung open to reveal her mom. She waved Vanessa down.

"Oh you're here! Good! I was worried about you taking a car with some stranger."

"Mom, it's a taxi. I didn't hitchhike."

"Still, I would prefer if you'd let your sister come and pick you up next time. Or, you know, your dad still says you can have his old truck."

Vanessa's eyes glanced over at the worn down truck her father had since she was twelve. It had one door that wouldn't open and the other door held on with some duct tape. If you weren't careful, it could pop right off, so to get into it you had to go in through a window.

"I'm okay. I already told Bradley she could drive me home tonight."

"Oh good! Much better."

Inside, Vanessa was greeted by her father. He wrapped his arms around her, hugging her tight. Vanessa squirmed beneath his touch and slid out from his hug. When she got away from his arms, her father looked hurt.

"Sorry. I just–it was tight."

"Come on in. Bradley should be here soon."

They went to sit in the living room, waiting for Bradley. Vanessa could smell dinner in the oven—lasagna, one of her mother's staple dishes. It made her stomach growl, and that's when she realized she hadn't eaten since breakfast.

"Do you need a snack?" her mother asked.

"No. I can wait until food is ready." She sighed and tucked her hands between her knees. She hoped Bradley would be here soon; she had no idea what to talk about with her parents.

"So, do you have any job prospects?" her father asked a beat later.

"Oh, um, I have a job interview tomorrow, actually."

"What type of interview?"

"I think it's a receptionist position," Vanessa said. She didn't miss the way her parents side eyed one another.

"Oh?" Her mother's voice rose at the end. "That-that sounds lovely. It's a bit different than you're used to, though, isn't it?"

"What's wrong with being a receptionist?"

"Absolutely nothing," her dad said. "Your mother was one before you were born, before she became a stay-at-home mother for you two girls."

"Whatever makes you happy, dear."

Vanessa's jaw tightened. They were patronizing her. Thankfully, Bradley walked before Vanessa could say anything about it.

As Bradley drove her sister home, she kept looking over at her. Vanessa's eyes remained on the window, and she hadn't said a word since they left their parents' place.

"Are you okay?" Bradley finally asked.

Vanessa lowly chuckled.

"Yep. Absolutely peachy."

"Why are you upset? Mom and Dad were cool about everything. They didn't drill you once about why you left without telling them or why you quit your job."

"Yes, because they've decided I'm having some sort of breakdown and are treating me with kid gloves."

"Well, I mean you kind of are," Bradley said, earning a scathing glare from Vanessa. "What? You are. There's nothing to be ashamed of, Ness. You've been through a lot."

Vanessa huffed, crossing her arms over her chest.

"I'm fine now," she stressed. "I'm getting my life back together. I have three interviews just this week. I have a place to live. I don't need to be treated any differently."

"Okay, fine. Good for you," Bradley deadpanned. Vanessa was becoming insufferable lately, with her mood swings that often swung deeper into anger than anything. But as she parked her car at Vanessa's apartment and turned to face her sister, she softened, feeling horrible for being irritated with her at all. Her cheeks were sunken in and pale, and there were unmistakable tears in her eyes. "Ness—"

"Thanks for the ride," Vanessa said, getting out of the car in a rush.

"You're going to see the therapist on Thursday, right?"

"Yes, of course I am. Goodnight." She shut the door and turned away. Bradley watched her sister go up the stairs and enter her apartment before pulling out of the parking lot.

Three interviews in two days. Every single one said she was either 'too qualified' or 'not what they were looking for.' She tugged the pins holding her hair up into a bun and placed them on the countertop. She didn't know where to look for a job next.

She left her bathroom and headed into the kitchen, dragging out the newest bottle of whiskey she'd bought the day before. Her phone dinged. It was likely her mother asking about the latest interview or her sister reminding her, yet again, about her therapy appointment tomorrow. Vanessa ignored them both.

The liquid now soothed her the moment it touched her tongue. She felt at ease; like she could survive anything as long as she had her whiskey. Vanessa sat down on the stool—one of the three places she had to sit on in her entire apartment—and kept drinking. There was no longer a nagging voice telling her she was being self-destructive. She'd been able to drink it away.

She glanced at the therapist appointment reminder on her fridge. Just a few days ago she was so sure she was going to go, but now with it a day away, she realized she couldn't do it. She didn't need it. Vanessa pulled her phone out, swiping all the messages away, and dialing the number for the therapist's office.

"Hello, Dr. Miles's office. How can I help you?"

"Um, yes, hello, this is Vanessa Price. I have an appointment with Dr. Miles tomorrow, but I am unable to make my appointment."

"Oh, I'm sorry to hear that, Ms. Price. Could we reschedule you to a later date? I see you're a new client. She's booked up for the next couple of weeks, but what about the 24th at 9?"

"No, I don't think I can make that either. Thank you, though."

"Are you sure?"

"Yes. Goodbye."

Before the man could say anything else on the other end, Vanessa hung up her phone. Without that appointment lingering over her head, she felt a weight fall off her shoulders. If she went to the therapy session, she knew the doctor would make her talk about what happened to her and go into detail over it. That was the last thing Vanessa wanted. She much preferred her own coping mechanism right now, which was burying it deep down inside of her and letting the golden liquid ease her fears. While some might disagree with her method of dealing with her trauma, she had to say it was working quite well for her.

Bradley had two nights off from work so she was traveling with friends to Atlanta. It had been too long since she'd done something this fun for herself. Addison would be picking her up in about ten minutes, just enough time for Bradley to check in with her sister.

"Hello?" Vanessa answered the phone, sounding half asleep.

"It's noon."

"And?"

"You're asleep."

"I don't have a job," Vanessa said, yawning. "Today's interview isn't until two."

"Okay. Well, you did go to your appointment yesterday, didn't you?"

"Appointment?"

Bradley tapped her hand against her thigh, frustration bubbling up within her.

"The therapy appointment. I worked hard to get you that."

"Um, yeah, of course I went," Vanessa replied.

"And how did it go?"

"Fine."

"You didn't go," Bradley said, shaking her head angrily. "You didn't go, did you?"

"Bradley—"

"You know what, if you want to destroy yourself, go for it. I have to go." Bradley slammed the end button and placed her phone into her purse. She took a moment to breathe through her anger and disappointment. For nearly a year, she'd been walking on eggshells around Vanessa and making sure she got what she needed so she didn't go off the deep end. Now, Bradley was done. She was going to enjoy her time away and not concern herself with what her sister was up to. Vanessa could figure it out on her own.

"We're sorry. The position was filled this morning," the woman told Vanessa when she handed her resume over to her.

"But my interview was for two," Vanessa said. "It's one forty-five."

"Yes, well, I'm sorry, they already filled the position. I can keep your resume for the future."

"Thanks," Vanessa said. She adjusted the strap of her purse over her shoulder and walked back out of the office.

Since she was downtown and had time to kill, Vanessa walked down the block, searching for a boutique to go into. Maybe she'd get her sister an 'I'm sorry I'm a screw up' gift. She headed toward a cute boutique right across the street when her eyes were drawn to the restaurant across the road. She knew it had a bar.

Yes, maybe a drink or two was just what she needed to handle her disappointment.

Right at six when Jones opened the doors to the bar, he was shocked to find Vanessa waiting on the other side. She was already unsteady on her feet, holding her black heels in her hands. His eyes glanced down at her bare feet on the filthy ground.

"You're going to cut your feet. People throw all sorts of things on the ground," he said, concerned.

Vanessa glanced around him.

"Where's my sister?"

"She's not working tonight," he said. He reached for her elbow, holding on to her to keep her from falling over. "Come on, why don't you let me take you home?" He was worried about her; he'd never seen her drunk before. Something told him this was more than just a couple of drinks and that she'd gotten herself like this to try and suppress her trauma.

"Nope. Not falling for that one again," Vanessa slurred. She pushed against him to make her way into the bar. "Who do I go to for a drink?"

Jones rushed behind her. "I'll get you some water."

"I didn't ask for water."

"Fine, coffee," Jones said, raising his brow. He'd been around Vanessa several times before tonight, but this was a very different Vanessa than he was used to. She was aggressive and brash, not the kind woman he'd spent time with just a while back.

Vanessa stumbled her way over toward the bar, taking a seat on one of the barstools, and requesting a whiskey from the bartender. Jones sighed.

"One drink," he said to Mads. "Don't give her anymore."

Vanessa scowled at him.

"I'm a grown woman," she said. "I can drink as much as I want."

Jones stared at her intently. Her hair had been in a bun, which was now part way down with hair in her face. Beneath her eyes were dark circles, and he couldn't determine if they were from lack of sleep or the alcohol, maybe both.

"You can't drink what you want in my bar," Jones finally said. "One drink."

Vanessa took her drink from Mads and turned so her back was to Jones. Hopefully he could get some food in her and then get her home safely. He decided he would keep an extra eye on her until then.

However, the night got away from him. For a weeknight, the bar was crowded. He lost sight of Vanessa after an hour and walked over to ask Mads where she was.

"Um, she went to another bar after I told her she couldn't have more to drink."

"Damnit," Jones said under his breath. Technically, Vanessa wasn't his responsibility. She was a grown woman who could do as she wished. But he still felt responsible for her. And he *wanted* her to be safe. "Watch the bar."

Jones went to the bar across the street, hoping he would find her there. He doubted she could make it too far alone. Fear consumed him and he glanced around on his walk to the next bar. What if she'd passed out, or worse—what if someone took advantage of her in this state? He quickened his steps.

Luckily, he spotted her right away in the bar. Vanessa sat, sipping on another glass of whiskey and kicking her bare feet. He went to her, getting in her view. She saw him and rolled her eyes.

"Why are you here?"

"Come on," he said, gently grabbing her upper arm. "It's time to go now, Vanessa. You've had your fun. Let me take you home."

Thankfully, everyone at this bar knew Jones and so they knew he wasn't some creep trying to take a random girl from the bar. Vanessa tugged her arm away from him, making her drink slosh in the glass.

"Leave me alone, Jones. I'm a big girl. I can do what I want." She leaned forward, losing her balance, and he could tell she was struggling to keep her eyes open.

"So you guys just let your patrons get so drunk they can pass out?" Jones questioned the bartender. He just shrugged. "Vanessa, come on."

"No. I like it better here. They let me drink."

"At my bar, I'll get you the special," Jones lied. He watched as Vanessa perked up.

"The special?"

"Yep. Come on."

She got out of her chair, nearly falling onto Jones. He had to hold her up as he led her back to his bar, hoping to find her shoes along the way.

"What's this special?" she asked the moment they made it into Lucky Ones.

"It's a ride home," Jones told her.

Vanessa shoved him away from her and growled.

"I don't need a ride home. I am fine! Who do you think you are?! You are not my boyfriend or even my friend! Leave me alone!" Every word was slurred and Vanessa struggled to keep herself upright.

"No."

Tired of her antics, Jones just picked her up. She fought, trying to hit him with her balled up fists.

"I'm not going to hurt you, Vanessa," he said. "I'm trying to help you."

He led her to the back room where he had a little lounge for his workers. It had a worn down couch, a coffee machine, and some snacks. Some of his workers would take catnaps in here during their short breaks during the night.

As they reached the lounge, he set her down.

"Where are your shoes?" he asked her.

"Who cares?"

"Whatever, I'm taking you home now."

"But you don't know where I live," Vanessa sang in a sing-songy voice. She swayed sharply to the left and Jones had to grab her hand to keep her from falling over.

"Vanessa, will you please tell me your address?" he asked as calmly as possible.

"No," she said sharply. "How do I know I can trust you?"

Jones inhaled. "I saved your sister from that creep several months ago. I just want to make sure you make it home safely."

"Hmm." She pondered, then bent over and before Jones had time to react, she vomited right onto his chest. Jones glanced down at the vomit covering his shirt and jeans.

"Great," he muttered to himself.

Vanessa stumbled more on her feet before ending up on the couch behind her. She laid down and tucked her hands beneath her cheek.

"I'm just going to lay here for a minute," she said. Jones took in a deep breath, watching her fall asleep. Tonight was going to be a long night.

Chapter Twenty-Three

Her head felt as though it was going to split open. Vanessa pressed her fingers firmly against her forehead and moaned.

"Here," she heard someone say to her. She quickly opened her eyes, trying to figure out who was in her apartment. But as her eyes tried to adjust to the brightness in the room, she realized she was not in her apartment. She wasn't on her air mattress. No, she was somewhere else. Her eyes widened; her body tensed.

"No, no, no," she whispered to herself, panic consuming her. This couldn't be happening again.

"Take it. You'll feel better," a familiar voice said. Vanessa turned her eyes to the voice and saw it was Jones holding a coffee and aspirin. Then she recognized the back room of Lucky Ones and realized she was fully clothed. Her heart settled. She was safe. Vanessa closed her eyes, and dug her head into the couch.

"What happened?" she croaked.

"You don't remember?"

"Not really," she said before it hit her. She groaned, feeling embarrassed, and tried to sit up. Jones sat the coffee down on the table in front of her and placed his hand on her shoulder.

"Don't overdo it. You had a lot to drink last night. I kept coming back here to check on you, worried you might choke on your vomit or something."

A fresh memory of her vomiting came through and she gasped.

"I threw up on you, didn't I?"

"Yes."

"Oh my god. I'm so sorry! I don't know what—and I was a brat too, wasn't I?"

"Well, you weren't exactly a ball of sunshine, but it's okay," Jones said with a chuckle.

"It's not," Vanessa disagreed. She grabbed the coffee, hoping it would help ease her headache.

"Here." He handed her the aspirin as well. "Give yourself a minute."

"So you stayed here all night?" Vanessa asked Jones. He nodded, rubbing the back of his neck. "I'm sorry. You shouldn't have had to watch me."

"I didn't mind it," Jones said. His eyes remained on her, never looking away.

"I'm just such a mess," Vanessa admitted, her voice catching in her throat. She felt her eyes watering and she had to look away from Jones's intense, worried gaze.

"It's okay."

"No, it's not okay," she whispered. "I've made Bradley give up on me. I can't face a day without a drink. Nothing is okay."

"First of all, your sister has not given up on you, she loves you. And second of all, admitting you have a problem is a good first step. How long have you been drinking?"

"I don't know, a while." She glanced back up at Jones. He remained with his eyes on her, full of compassion and grace. There wasn't any judgement staring back at her. "Everything got worse after Bradley was drugged. It's like it—"

"Triggered you?"

"Yes," Vanessa breathed. "I had been doing alright before that and then I started doing better after I moved to New York too. I told myself it would be my fresh start, but things kept happening to bring it back up, no matter how much I tried to bury it."

"It would have come eventually. If not then, weeks later, maybe years, but you couldn't keep it buried for long."

"Why not?" Vanessa cried.

"Because it doesn't work like that, Vanessa. I'm sorry you've gone through this. I'm sorry the pain has caused you to feel like you need to harm yourself to make it through each day."

Vanessa blinked, allowing a few tears to fall down her face. She leaned forward before a sob overtook her, feeling Jones's arm wrap around her shoulders and pull her to his chest. She felt safe; secure there in his embrace—safe enough to sob until there were no more tears to cry.

"Do you need me to walk you to your door?" Jones asked. Vanessa sat in the passenger seat, gnawing anxiously on the corner of her thumb. He reached over to pull her hand away from her mouth, meeting her eyes. "Would you like to go get something to eat instead of staying here alone?"

"No," Vanessa whispered. "I think I should go home and rest a bit."

"And throw out the alcohol under the sink," Jones said pointedly. Vanessa's cheeks turned bright red.

"I wasn't like this before."

Jones's face softened. "I know you weren't, and there's nothing to be embarrassed about, Vanessa. People are allowed to fumble, what's important is getting back up on your feet."

"Right," Vanessa answered with a shaky breath. "I don't know what would have happened to me had you not come and gotten me from the other bar. I was an idiot."

"Don't do that to yourself. I was there."

Vanessa gave him a nod. She reached over, hugging him and holding onto him tightly. Jones hugged her back.

"Thank you," she whispered into his ear. Then she pulled back and stepped out of the car. She wore some fuzzy socks which had been the only thing Jones could find at the corner store to give her feet some protection.

"Call me if you need me."

"I will."

She waved at him, tucking her hair behind her ear. She gave him a tentative smile and turned to go upstairs. Jones watched her until she went into her apartment, wishing he'd gone with her.

As he began pulling out of the parking lot, his phone started ringing. It was Bradley. After Vanessa passed out, he'd messaged her to let her know.

"I just got your messages. Is Vanessa okay?"

"Yes. I just dropped her off at her place."

There was a pause. "She spent the night with you?"

"She spent the night in the lounge at the bar," Jones said. "She woke up pretty hungover, but she's alright."

"Maybe I should come back today."

"No, don't do that. Vanessa wouldn't want you to. You can call her and check in, if you want, but stay and have fun. You can see her when you get back."

"Are you sure she's all right? Getting black out drunk isn't her at all."

"Well, she told me—" Jones debated telling Bradley. It wasn't his business to tell, but he also thought it might be best for Vanessa to have extra support. "She's been drinking daily, just to make it through the day."

"Oh," Bradley said sadly on the other end. "Right, well, thanks for telling me. Um, thank you for watching over her last night. I appreciate it, Jones. Truly."

"It wasn't a problem. I'm just glad I was there."

"Me too," Bradley said. "I guess I should get going. Thanks again."

Once he placed his phone down, he glanced back up at Vanessa's apartment. He was so glad he'd been there to help her the night before. He couldn't imagine what could have happened had he not been. His hands tightened around his steering wheel as he struggled with the feelings within himself about Vanessa. She clearly was not in a good place, so he shouldn't even give these thoughts the time of day. Plus, there was Bradley. He shook his head, knowing this was way too complicated and that it was best to push all it away.

Vanessa got a text from Bradley a couple days later stating she was coming over. It wasn't a request; it was a fact. Vanessa was anxious of what her sister had to say. She was sure Jones had told Bradley all about her escapades the other night. Just thinking about it made her cheeks burn with embarrassment. She wasn't prepared for the wrath that was likely to come through her front door.

Her sister arrived moments later, walking in through Vanessa's unlocked door. Vanessa remained stuck in her spot on the stool in her kitchen.

"Hi," she meekly said.

Bradley walked into the apartment, placing a bag down on Vanessa's kitchen counter. She glanced at her sister before pulling something out of the bag. As she lifted it out, Vanessa saw a flowery notebook with a pen tied to it with a pale pink ribbon. Bradley placed it into Vanessa's hands.

"This is for you," Bradley said.

Vanessa turned the notebook over, wondering what motivated her sister to give this gift to her. She definitely hadn't deserved anything.

"It's beautiful."

"I thought," Bradley started carefully, "that perhaps you could use a different, healthier outlet. You've always been a brilliant writer, so that's why I thought a notebook might be a good idea."

"Thank you," Vanessa said. "I thought you'd come here to yell at me. I'm sure Jones told you—"

Bradley lifted her hand to stop her sister from saying anything else. She shook her head.

"Look, I'm sorry I got irritated with you. It wasn't really fair of me."

"Oh, it absolutely was," Vanessa said. "You had every right." Vanessa undid the ribbon that secured the pen to the notebook and twirled it with her fingers. "I do want to be happy, Bradley."

"I know you do." Her eyes scanned the kitchen, searching for something.

"I poured them all out," Vanessa said, knowingly. "Go on. You can search everywhere. I kept them under the sink."

"I trust you."

"Go on," Vanessa repeated, "look."

Bradley took the offer and began her search around the kitchen, opening every door and cabinet. After she finished in there, she checked the closets and bags in Vanessa's apartment. Since she didn't have any actual furniture yet, it left little room for hiding places.

"Good for you," Bradley said. "Was it hard?"

"Yes," Vanessa confessed. "I did save myself one glass of whiskey before pouring it all out. I drank a little bit until it was gone." She placed the pen down on top of the notebook and started bouncing her knees. "I just don't know what I'm doing anymore, Bradley."

"Well, I have a possible option for you. I was speaking to Addison about her mom's bookshop and she needs someone to work fulltime starting next week."

"Huh," Vanessa pondered.

"I mean, you like books. You could be around them all day. It could help with your creativity."

"Yeah, I mean, I do need a job. Are you sure she'll want me?"

"Addison told her mom, who said she'd give you a day to decide."

"Then, yes, sure."

"And I have one more thing for you," Bradley said. She pulled Vanessa's manuscript out of the bag and placed it next to the notebook. "Publish this."

"Bradley, no. I only wrote it for fun."

"No, you wrote it because it inspired you. You wrote it to add something to this world, and it's amazing, Nessa. The world deserves to see it. I can't force you to publish it, but I do think you should try. And you should keep writing. Let that side of yourself flourish. Stop hiding it away."

Vanessa lifted the manuscript into her hands. Just holding it made her feel whole. She'd spent over a year working on this piece of art. She brought it up to her chest and hugged it.

"Will you go to therapy now?" Bradley asked.

"Yes," Vanessa said. "I will. I'm so embarrassed. I don't know if I'll ever be able to face Jones again. Did he tell you I threw up on him?"

"What?" Bradley asked, her eyes wide. "No! You did not!"

"I did!"

"Wow," Bradley exclaimed.

"Yeah, not sure I can get any worse than that," Vanessa mused. She felt her cheeks reddening as she remembered what she'd done.

"I surely hope not!" Bradley exclaimed with a smile.

"Me either."

CHAPTER TWENTY-FOUR

Vanessa walked down a hallway she used to walk down several times a week. So many random items around the office made old memories come back. The disproportionally large clock on the wall reminded her of a time she and Grey made out after everyone else had gone home. He'd caught her by surprise, pressing her up against the wall and next to the clock. They'd both giggled before he'd kissed her.

She swallowed hard. There was his door, with his name carved in letters on the plaque. She reached out, allowing her fingers to run over every letter—something she used to do when he was in the middle of an important phone call and she didn't want to interrupt. Today, she did it to put off the inevitable.

When her finger hit the last letter of his last name, she curled her hand into a fist and knocked on the door.

"Come in!" Grey's voice called out. Her heart skipped a beat; she wanted to turn and run out of the office.

She didn't. She turned the handle and stood in the doorway. Grey's eyes widened at the sight of her before he stood from his chair.

"Nessa," he breathed. "What—I thought you lived in New York."

"Not anymore. That was temporary. Can I speak with you for a moment?"

"Of course." Grey pointed to a chair and told her to sit down. She did as she was asked. He pulled a chair closer to the one where Vanessa sat, now sitting where their knees almost touched.

Vanessa's palms grew sweaty; her breathing grew labored. She didn't want to do this, but deep down, she knew he deserved to know the truth. Grey reached across and touched her hand, giving it a loving squeeze.

"What's the matter?"

"Everything," Vanessa whispered. It felt surreal to say that out loud to him. "I need to tell you the truth about what happened. It's only fair to you. You may hate me when you find out, but, well, I can't keep lying to you just because I'm afraid of how you'll react."

"I don't think I could ever hate you, Nessa."

"You don't know that." Vanessa shuddered. She closed her eyes, transporting back to that fateful night. "It all started that evening we went to dinner with your friend, Liam."

As Vanessa told Grey about that night, she'd avoided his gaze. When she reached the end, she finally gathered the courage to look at him. His face was flushed red, his jaw clenched, and there was a deep crease on his forehead.

"I'm sorry," Vanessa whispered. Grey shot up from his seat, bringing his hand up into the air. Instinctively, she sat back.

"You have *nothing* to apologize for, Nessa. Nothing!" The anger in his voice startled Vanessa, making her cry. He quickly lowered his voice. "Please don't cry." He eased back into his chair and touched her knee. "Nessa, *please* don't cry."

"I ruined everything." She covered her face, slouching her shoulders forward. "I should have done something differently."

"No," Grey said strongly. "You did nothing wrong. He did. He took advantage of you and then tried to make you out as the one who did something wrong. I just—I don't understand why you wouldn't tell me."

"I was scared. I still am," Vanessa admitted. "And I believed him at first, that I initiated it. I think it was easier in a way, than believing what really happened. It all blew up in my face, though. I lost everything. I lost my job. I lost the house. I lost myself. I lost you." The last three words came out wobbly on her tongue. Grey stared at her intensely. "I-I'm not here trying to get you back or anything like that. I know you have Emma and that you love her."

At the mention of Emma's name, Grey smiled that goofy smile which showed just how in love he truly was.

"I do."

"I'm glad for you." She sniffled. "Truly, I am. I just want you to be happy, Grey."

Grey inched forward, taking her hand in his own.

"You know I'll always love you, right?" he asked. "You will always hold a special place in my heart, Nessa. I want you to find happiness, too."

"Right now I'm just trying to find out who I am." She wiped beneath her eye with her finger.

"I want to find Liam and kill him," Grey said, under his breath.

"Well, don't do that. You'll get yourself in trouble. But don't let him anywhere near Emma, and tell everyone you know about what a creep he is."

"I never should have left you alone with him," Grey said, regretfully. "I should have protected you."

Vanessa blinked back the tears.

"It wasn't your fault, Grey."

"And it wasn't yours, either." He pressed a kiss to her cheek. "I hope you know that."

Vanessa gave him a crooked smile. She brushed her hand against his cheek.

"I do love you, Grey. I always will."

Chapter Twenty-Five

T he bookshop was peaceful. It sat on the corner of a street in Downtown Savannah. Even though it wasn't very large, it had plenty of customers each day, because it had been in the town for over twenty years. The old brick building had a welcoming feeling every time you stepped in and were immersed by the warm colors and books on the shelves.

Vanessa knew it was only for now, but it was a good way to get her feet back into life. Here she found happiness in her days. She helped people find books and spent her days placing books on bookshelves or looking through inventory. If there was a lull in her day, she could sit on the large, lush chair by the window and read or write in her notebook. Something about this place was magical.

Vanessa was in the middle of writing a sentence when the bell of the door dinged. She jumped up from her seat, hiding the notebook beneath the chair, and looked up at the new customer. It was Jones. Upon noticing Vanessa, he smiled.

"Has Bradley sent you here to spy on me?" Vanessa asked. Jones's smile grew, making his eyes brighten and the skin around his eyes crinkle. She was glad to see things weren't going to be awkward between them after what happened a few weeks prior.

"No, I didn't even know you worked here." Jones pulled out his wallet and showed Vanessa the punch card every customer got with their purchase—twenty punches, five dollars off. "I've been a regular here since I moved to Savannah."

"Oh, cool. Well, do you need help finding a book? Let me guess, history books are your thing?"

"Actually, I'm a fan of romances."

"Oh! I'll have to let Bradley know," Vanessa teased, not missing the way Jones's cheeks blushed slightly.

"Maybe, don't. She already gets a laugh by calling me Teddy all the time."

"Why would she call you that?" Vanessa asked, not understanding.

"Because my name is Ted. Has she not told you?"

"No," Vanessa said. She eyed Jones from head to toe, pondering his name. "Huh, Ted Jones. Nice, solid name. But I think Jones suits you best."

"Thank you. Try telling your sister that."

Vanessa laughed. "Bradley does things her own way. Alright, romance. I'm guessing you know where it is?"

"I do," Jones said.

"Well, enjoy looking around."

Vanessa waited until Jones went further back into the store to sit back down and get back to her writing. She appreciated Mrs. Latham's easy nature about the job. She didn't mind Vanessa sitting while other customers were inside as long as they got what they needed and she was up when they were ready to check out.

"What are you writing?" Jones asked when he came back shortly with several books stacked high in his arms.

"Nothing." Vanessa put her notebook back in its hiding place. She took the books from Jones and began scanning them at the register. Some were romance, others were history (so she had been right), and some were thrillers. "It seems you like a good variety of stories."

"I do. What's your favorite?"

About a year ago, Vanessa would have answered with some answer that sounded sophisticated, trying to fit the mold she felt she needed to stay within, but today she answered truthfully.

"Fantasy. When I pick up a good fantasy book, I get so lost within it that I can't put it down. Sometimes, I'll forgo sleep for a good book."

"Well, isn't that what you're supposed to do?" Jones asked, tilting his head slightly.

"I think so," Vanessa said. "I, um," she paused. "I actually wrote a fantasy book. Silly, isn't it?"

"Why would that be silly?" His question was genuine. "I think that's amazing. Are you going to publish it?"

"I don't know. Bradley says I should. But what if…what if no one likes it?" The thought of putting her words out there for someone else to read frightened her.

"I can tell you this: you write for yourself, right?"

"Yes."

"You write to tell a story that matters to you, right?"

"Of course."

"Then if you put it out in the world, I'd be willing to bet someone will like it. It won't be for everyone, but that's why there are so many genres of books. What's your story about?"

Vanessa chewed on the inside of her cheek.

"You really want to know?" she asked in awe. He grinned at her, making her heart skip a beat.

"Absolutely."

They talked for close to an hour, Vanessa giving him details about her book and all the characters within it. It wasn't until the bell of the door jingled that she realized how caught up they were in their conversation.

"We'll chat more later," Jones said, giving her a wink that made her swoon. She watched him as he exited the store before remembering she had a new customer. The customer had walked right past her and into the aisles. She could have spoken to Jones longer.

She made a sound, and shook her head. What was she thinking? Bradley had a crush on Jones. Surely, she didn't like Jones—not like that, did she? Jones was just her…friend. Vanessa pondered that word. She sunk into the chair by the window and sighed. She felt much more for Jones than friendship. But she wouldn't do anything about it. No, it wouldn't be right for her to want to spend time with him like this. Her sister had done so much for her this past year, it wouldn't be fair for her to like a guy she liked.

Bradley unlocked the door to her apartment. It was nearing two in the morning, a bit earlier than usual for getting home after a shift at Lucky Ones. She yawned, kicking off her shoes over into a corner. Then she started taking off her earrings and placing them in the little dish next to her sink before washing her face. As she splashed the water against her skin, her phone rang. She twisted her lips. Who would be calling her at this hour?

She walked over to search for her phone in her purse to find Vanessa calling her.

"Hello?"

"I couldn't sleep," Vanessa said, her voice quiet.

"Are you okay?"

"Yes. I think."

"Do you need me to come over?" Bradley went in search of her shoes, ready to put them back on.

"No, I shouldn't have even called."

"Don't be ridiculous. You can call me day or night, any time. What happened?"

"Well, I had my first therapy session today, and it…it was good. She's nice and helpful, but talking about everything has brought things up I've been pushing away. And now I want to drink."

"But you didn't?" Bradley asked, holding her breath.

"No. I haven't."

Bradley let out a breath of air, so glad to hear it.

"Good."

"Bradley, I see him every time I close my eyes." She heard her sister cry.

"Why don't I sit up with you for a while? We can talk about whatever you need. Do you want to talk about what you spoke about today in therapy?"

"No."

"What about work? How'd your first week go?"

"Good, really good. I love it there. I actually started working on a sequel for my manuscript during my free time."

"Oh yeah? What happens next?"

For the next half an hour or so, Vanessa told Bradley about her new story. There was actual joy in her sister's voice. She was finding herself again.

"Alright, I should go to bed. I have to be at the shop at ten, which will be here before I know it. Thanks for staying up with me. I love you."

"I love you too. Goodnight, Ness."

"Back so soon?" Vanessa asked as she worked on adjusting some of the toys in the children's section of the bookstore. A mom with her three children had just come in and the children had a blast playing over there. The mom tried to clean up after them, but Vanessa told her it would be no bother in doing it herself.

"Well, I needed the second book in a series I got last week," Jones said. Vanessa felt her chest grow warm, thrilled to know she'd be seeing Jones more here in the bookstore.

"Oh? What kind of book was it?"

"History," he said.

"A history book series?"

"Yes."

Vanessa led him back to the history section, as though he had no idea where it could be. Her fingers ran over the spines of some of the books, lifting one to look at the cover.

"So which series of books is it?"

"There," Jones pointed. He grabbed two more books. "It's a three parter about Roman history. I should have gotten them all when I came in last week, but I thought it would take me longer to get through the first."

"Are you interested in Roman history?"

"Yes, but really any and all history."

"And what's your favorite type of romance?" she asked, finding any reason to learn more about Jones.

"Any with a happy ending," Jones said.

"Happy endings are definitely nice. It's good to get out of the real world for a bit, isn't it?"

"Well, I believe happy endings can happen."

"You do?" Vanessa asked, skeptically. "Really?"

"Of course, I do. Don't you?"

Vanessa's shoulders tightened and she began to rub her hands together.

"I don't know, not anymore."

Jones looked her directly in the eyes, a sympathetic look staring back at her.

"I do hope one day you will again."

"Me too. But for now, I'm just searching out moments that make me happy," Vanessa said. "My therapist says that happiness doesn't have to be some big huge moment, it can be the little things."

"And has anything made you happy today, Vanessa?" The way Jones stared into her soul made Vanessa's chest tighten. She could feel his name trying to tumble off her tongue, but she swallowed it back.

"Yes. Today has been a good day."

"I'm glad to hear it."

Jones grabbed the newer books from the backseat of his car and walked inside the bar. It was getting close to lunchtime and he needed to get the last-minute menu details settled. He placed the bag on the counter before heading to the back, where he saw Bradley sneaking a snack out of the fridge. She gave him a sheepish smile and grabbed an extra slice of cheese to give to him.

"Why are you here so early? And where's Mads?"

"He ran out back to get something, why?"

"Just have to make sure the menu is good for today's lunch."

He munched on the cheese and decided to go back up front to work on prepping other things for lunchtime. Bradley followed behind him before pausing at the bag of books.

"Whose are these?"

"Mine," Jones answered. He grabbed the bag, but Bradley grabbed it as well and peeked inside.

"Right, you're a reader."

"Big reader," he said. "I have a whole wall of books upstairs in my apartment."

"Cool. Wait, this is from the store where Vanessa works. Did you see her there? Did you talk to her?"

Thinking of Vanessa made his body feel light. Every time he'd run into her this past week, he'd been excited to spend that time with her. He found he could talk to her for hours.

"Yes, I did talk to her."

"Oh," Bradley said. "And what did you talk about?"

"Not much, books mainly. She told me about this story she's written. It sounds pretty cool."

"She told you about her manuscript?" Bradley asked, surprised. "She doesn't tell anyone about that, except me."

"Well, she did tell me. Are you jealous?" Jones teased her.

"No," Bradley said, "not at all." She stood there for a moment with a thoughtful expression on her face. Her mouth opened, looking up at him before she closed it, deciding not to say whatever was on her mind. Then she grabbed her towel and walked out of the room.

Chapter Twenty-Six

Once a month Sunday brunches with Mom were back. She'd only been back to Georgia for about a month, and her mother was demanding their brunches to return. Bradley had been invited, as well, but she had the excuse of working too late at night.

Even though things had been turning around for her, Vanessa wasn't looking forward to this one-on-one time with her mom. She still had a lot to work through in therapy; she still had nightmares and thoughts of running away. Writing did help, though. Her sister had been right about it being a better outlet for her grief and trauma.

"You look so much better!" her mother said the moment she saw her outside. Her mother walked toward her, wrapping her arm around her shoulders and pulling her in for a hug. "The color is back in your cheeks! That new job must be good for you."

"I do like it," Vanessa said. "I get to read books and talk to customers. It's a lot less stressful than my old job."

"But I bet the pay is a lot less," her mother added, raising a brow.

"Yes, it is a lot less, but I have less expenses now. It won't be a long-term job, but it works for me while I figure everything else out."

"And do you have any plans for the future?"

They were taken to their regular booth. Her mother slid in first and then Vanessa did the same.

"No," Vanessa said. "I have zero plans. Right now, I'm just working on me."

"And what is that you need to work on, exactly," her mother prodded. "You never did tell me."

Vanessa inhaled. "Just myself. I wasn't happy at my old job."

"But people don't work to be happy, Vanessa. They work to make money. You worked hard to get where you were. If you'd stuck with it, in a few years, you could have gotten promoted and maybe done something that did make you happy."

"I'm sorry," Vanessa whispered. "I'm sorry I'm not the daughter you thought I was, Mom, but that job was killing me. My life was killing me. I needed to change to get better." Vanessa couldn't believe she, the people pleaser, had just said that out loud. But it had needed to be said—she had been slowly killing herself, losing all the light within her that was Vanessa.

When she looked up, she saw a stunned and concerned look upon her mother's features. Her mom's jaw was open and she reached out to touch Vanessa's hand.

"What on earth caused you such pain?"

Vanessa shook her head. She couldn't tell her mother or anyone else the truth of what happened.

"I just couldn't work there anymore."

"Tell me about Grey," Dr. Miles said. She sat in a large, green chair across from Vanessa, holding the small notebook where she took notes during each session.

"There's not much to say about him. I think I summed it up well enough at our last appointment. He and I were dating. I thought I cheated on him. I broke up with him. That's that."

"You said you dated him for three years?"

"Yes."

"And you had plans of getting engaged?"

"Yes," Vanessa said. She shifted in her seat, growing uncomfortable in this conversation. She'd hoped to move past her thoughts on Grey and everything that happened to their relationship after the assault.

"That must be hard, seeing him with someone else now and engaged. It's only been what, around a year since you broke it off?"

"I'm not jealous," Vanessa informed her. "Truly I'm not. He found someone he loves and they decided not to wait. Why should that make me upset?"

"Well, you were supposed to be engaged to him," Dr. Miles said. "You said in your last session that you still love him."

"I do. He loves me too. But since that night, our lives have gone on different paths, different journeys. The road broke off into two directions then and it never came back together."

"That's very metaphorical of you, Vanessa, but that doesn't negate how you feel about him."

"I know that, but I've come to terms with it as best I can. It did destroy me, but not facing what happened to me destroyed me more. I can find peace about Grey, because he did find someone else. Sometimes, it makes me think we weren't really meant to be, but that we'll always hold a place in one another's hearts for the other. A first real love sort of thing." She let out a breath, thinking of Grey. She still recalled the goofy grin on his face when she asked him if he loved Emma. It did hurt, but it also healed. He would be okay.

"I'm glad you've found some peace when it comes to Grey."

Vanessa nodded. "Oh! I wanted to tell you something."

"And what is that," Dr. Miles said with a smile.

"I stood up for myself to my mother. I was proud of that. I didn't expect my voice to come so soon in my healing, but it did. She was harping about my old job and I flat out told her I had to leave the job because it was killing me. I managed to tell her what I needed to do for my own healing, set a boundary, and also not tell her everything."

"Wow that is amazing. You're doing great, Vanessa."

"But not perfect."

Dr. Miles leaned forward, pulling her glasses off her nose and setting them on the table before her.

"Vanessa, it will never be perfect. You may have several weeks like this where everything seems like it's falling in place, but then hit a wall and you think none of your progress mattered, that you're back to square one. That's why you need tools for when those times come, because they will."

Bradley met her sister at Lucky Ones for lunch. She had been worried about Vanessa hanging out in a bar near alcohol, but Vanessa assured her she could be around it.

Vanessa sat across from her in a tee shirt and jeans with her hair pulled into a French braid. Sometimes she was so effortlessly beautiful it hurt.

"Five weeks in therapy. How does it feel?"

"Good," Vanessa said. "My therapist said I'm making great strides, but to prepare for setbacks. My progress is happening quickly, maybe too quickly. I don't know."

"I'm sure everyone heals at a different pace, Ness. Have you been sleeping any better?"

The space between Vanessa's eyes narrowed before she reluctantly shook her head.

"So as you see, maybe it's just outer healing," Vanessa said.

"Healing is healing. It won't happen overnight."

"No, it won't. Do you think I made the wrong choice by not reporting him? If another girl gets attacked, is it my fault?"

"What that bastard does is not on you, and you were right, sadly. You don't have enough proof. It is a he said, she said situation," Bradley said sadly.

"Which most cases are." Vanessa huffed. "It doesn't seem right, does it? And even when the man admits to what he does, we hear of cases over and over where he gets a simple slap on the wrist."

"No, it isn't right at all, but dwelling on that can't be good for you," Bradley replied. She was proud of Vanessa and the steps she'd taken, but it didn't keep Bradley from worrying she might fall back into bad habits.

"Probably not," Vanessa agreed. She glanced around the bar. "Where's Jones?"

"He took the day off, why?"

Vanessa shrugged. "No reason."

"Huh," Bradley said, eyeing her sister suspiciously. She noticed the small blush of her sister's cheeks and the disappointment on her face of Jones not being there.

"How are things between the two of you? Has he kissed you, yet?" Vanessa couldn't seem to meet her eyes as she asked this question.

"No, actually. I don't think it's like that between us."

"Oh?" There was no missing the hint of hope in her sister's eye. She quickly covered it up, frowning slightly. "Why not?"

"I think we're just friends, is all."

"I just assumed—did something happen? This isn't because you've had to deal with me, is it?" Vanessa asked.

"No, nothing like that," Bradley assured her. "Nothing happened, it's just that we aren't compatible like that."

"I'm sorry."

"Don't be. And let's be honest, I'm not really looking into settling down any time soon. I like keeping my options open."

Vanessa laughed at that, making Bradley smile. She was glad to see glimpses of her sister returning to her.

As the weeks continued to pass, Vanessa became more and more comfortable in her skin. It was only at night when it would creep up on her and she'd struggle to fall asleep or stay asleep without nightmares. Dr. Miles offered her some suggestions for better sleep, but none of them worked. Sometimes this would lead her to want to drink. She'd even gone into the liquor shop down the road, nearly buying some more whiskey. However, she was determined not to fall back on that clutch. She needed to figure out nighttime on her own.

There were nights she would call her sister, but she tried to avoid that. It wasn't fair to expect her to answer her calls in the middle of the night, even if she was awake.

Tonight, she was trying journaling. Her therapist suggested writing down her feelings before going to bed. She bought herself a plain blue journal, not wanting her fantasy writing and journaling to be in the same space. She wrote down Liam's name. It was something she was trying as a way to not to give his name power. But as she looked at the letters on the page, it made her feel ill. She scribbled over it with her pen until that space was a near blob. Then she closed the journal. Perhaps it would work another night.

Vanessa turned on the television. She knew studies showed she was more likely to get a better night's sleep by not having any screens on before bed, but she needed to get her mind off everything. And like most nights, it worked. She eventually fell asleep to the sound of an infomercial.

Of course, she was up hours later, not getting nearly enough sleep, but it was better than none at all.

Bradley nearly fell over when her parents showed up at her work. While they had shown up a while back, they hadn't returned since. She made sure they got a booth and brought them both over their favorite drinks.

"We wanted to thank you," her father said.

"And you had to come to my work to do that?" Bradley asked.

"No, we just wanted to see you."

"Oh, okay, and wait, why are you thanking me?" Bradley questioned as she tried to recall the last time her parents had ever thanked her for anything.

"Your sister seems so much better, Bradley, and we know you had a hand in it," her mother said. She narrowed her eyes. "Though I don't suppose you'll tell me what exactly made her stumble as she did. I'm not buying her story that it was her job. She worked there for years!"

"Mom," Bradley sighed. "I'm not getting involved in any of that. But I didn't do anything she wouldn't do for me. We're sisters. We love one another."

"Jones!" Her mother called out over Bradley to wave him over.

"Oh, Mr. and Mrs. Price, what brings you by tonight?"

"Just here to see our youngest. How have you been?"

As her parents caught up with Jones, Bradley walked away. She had other customers who needed her attention. She headed to the bar, needing a new pen. It seemed they always disappeared throughout the night.

Since she was near her phone, she checked her screen, surprised to find several texts from Vanessa. She lifted her phone to read them.

Grey called me. Liam's been arrested for alleged assault of another girl.

I don't know what to do.

What do I do?

Sorry, I know you're at work.

This is all my fault.

Bradley's heart raced in her chest. She needed to get to her sister now, but she didn't know how to leave without drawing suspicion from her parents. She couldn't very well tell them that their eldest daughter was having a panic attack, or else they would want to know why and what happened.

Jones was finally back and working at another table, so she made her way to him.

"Vanessa is having a bad night, but I can't alert my parents. Do you think you could come up with an excuse of why I had to go? Also, can I go?" she asked.

"Of course you can go," Jones said. "Is she all right? Does she need anything?" He bit down on his lower lip, obviously concerned about her sister.

"I think so." Bradley bounced on her heels, anxious. "I need to make sure."

"Right. I can cover for you. Go on. Check on Vanessa."

Bradley watched him for a moment, the puzzle pieces coming together clearer. But then she realized she didn't have time to ponder any of that. Vanessa needed her now.

She snuck out the back of the bar and went straight to her car. She tried to call her sister, but she didn't pick up.

When she reached her sister's apartment, she headed up to her apartment and knocked on the door, thankful when it opened a beat later. Vanessa looked pale, but she hadn't been crying.

"Hey," Bradley started. "How are you?" She groaned at herself. That was a stupid thing to ask.

"I'm okay. Part of me wishes Grey hadn't called me. I feel…numb?" Vanessa twisted her lips thoughtfully. "Like, I'm pleased he's been arrested, but that girl got hurt because I didn't say anything."

"No, this isn't your fault, Vanessa."

"Do I go to the police now?"

"If you want," Bradley said. "It could make the girl's case stronger. You could help put him away."

"Do you actually think they'll put him away? How can they prove we're even telling the truth?" Vanessa began to chew on the edge of her thumb.

"Maybe you shouldn't decide tonight. How about we order some pizza and watch a movie, what about that?"

Vanessa blinked harshly, and now Bradley could see the tears in her eyes.

"I was doing better."

"You *are* doing better, Ness. You are."

For several days after her breakdown, Bradley came over to the house to visit her and check in. Vanessa managed to convince her sister today that she was doing better so Bradley would stop coming by. While she appreciated her sister's concern, she didn't want her sister to have to worry about her anymore.

However, maybe she should have been, because Vanessa had been sitting at a bar for over an hour now, staring at the glass in front of her. She hadn't touched it; not yet. Despite what she'd told Bradley, she wasn't alright. Nights were harder, waking up was harder, everything was harder since Grey told her about Liam.

She was supposed to call her therapist when she felt herself sliding back. It was part of her plan for making healthy choices. Right now, though, she didn't feel like making healthy choices.

"I was told you were here." Vanessa looked up to see Jones. He slid into the barstool beside her.

"Why?" Vanessa asked. She lifted the glass, having no intentions of sipping it.

"The bartender called me after what happened in here last time," he said, pointing to the man behind the bar.

"Oh, right." Vanessa shook the cup, watching the golden liquid splash against the sides. "I'm not causing a scene this time."

"I see that."

"Then I don't need you to be here," Vanessa said. "Does Bradley know?"

"No, I didn't tell her."

"Good. It's best if you don't."

"Do you want to talk about why you are here, sitting in a bar, staring at a glass of alcohol?"

"No," Vanessa said. "It's not illegal, is it? I'm allowed to have a drink now and then, aren't I?"

"Yes, you are. But should you?"

Vanessa inhaled sharply, setting the glass back down onto the bar.

"I don't know, honestly. Probably not. Using alcohol as a coping mechanism isn't exactly therapist approved."

"What is therapist approved?"

"Um, writing in my journal, calling her, talking to someone."

"Well, I'm here. Talk to me."

Vanessa wiped her finger beneath her eye and let out a low chuckle.

"The guy who—" She shook her head. "Apparently, another girl said he did the same thing to her and took it to the police. I don't know if I should do the same."

"Ah."

"What do you think I should do?"

Jones thoughtfully stroked his chin before answering. "I can't tell you what to do, Vanessa. You are the only one who can make that choice, and no one should try to convince you in one way or the other. I certainly won't be."

Vanessa sighed. She appreciated that he wasn't pressuring her, but it also didn't make this any easier.

"What does your gut tell you to do?" Jones asked, leaning a bit closer to her.

"Make a report," Vanessa said, turning her hands in her lap. "But what if they don't believe me?"

"All you can control is what you do, Vanessa, not them." He paused a beat before adding, "I believe you."

"Would you go with me?"

"Of course."

CHAPTER TWENTY-SEVEN

Vanessa rested her head on Bradley's shoulder. After she went to the police station, Bradley got a call from her asking her to come over. She'd come right away, worried her sister might have gotten back into the whiskey. But she found her with ice cream instead; a much healthier coping mechanism.

"Were you nervous?" Bradley asked. She remembered when she'd gone to the station all that time ago, how nerve wracking it'd been.

"Yes, very, but Jones was with me," Vanessa said.

"Oh? I didn't realize…" Bradley's brows furrowed. "Did you invite him to come along?"

"I…I went to a bar and he found me there. Well, actually the bartender called him. I didn't drink anything," Vanessa clarified. "Anyway, I didn't want to go alone and he was there and…yeah."

"Oh," Bradley said quietly again. Again the puzzle pieces were coming into place. Vanessa and Jones. How had she missed it? She wasn't quite sure how she felt about that. Did *they* even realize it?

"What?" Vanessa asked, sitting up.

"Nothing," Bradley replied. "I'm glad you had someone to go with you. I would have gone."

"I know you would have, but I needed to go right then and Jones was there."

"Right," Bradley said. "And you called me right after."

"I did. Are you angry with me?"

"What? No," Bradley said, shaking her head. "Of course, not. Why would I be angry?"

"Because I was spending time with Jones."

Bradley didn't answer, her eyes lingered on the television screen. Vanessa and Jones. *Vanessa and Jones.*

"Bradley…"

"I'm not angry, Ness," Bradley said, sitting up straighter. She realized she wasn't, not at all. "Also, Jones doesn't belong to me, anyway, so I don't know what you're implying."

"Okay," Vanessa said, sighing. She placed her head back on her sister's shoulder. "I love you, Bradley. You've really been my rock this year."

Bradley's lips kissed the top of Vanessa's head.

"I love you too."

"What if we did a karaoke night?" Bradley suggested.

"No," Jones said, "absolutely not. I don't want to listen to people screech all night in the bar, especially drunk people who think they sound great."

"You're no fun," Bradley said. "Come on, karaoke nights would be a hit. We could put a small stage over in that corner, set up a microphone and everything."

"Don't care, I'm not doing karaoke here."

"What about an open mic night?" Mads suggested from the bar.

"Oh! Yes! Open mic night! You could have people sign up to sing, and bands." Bradley walked over to the corner, waving her arms around excitedly.

"Where would we even find people?" Jones asked, not buying it.

"I don't know. I'm sure we could figure it out. Make flyers or put something on the bar's website. You do have a website don't you?"

"Website? Why would I need a website?" Jones asked.

"Wow, I guess I need to set one of those up for you too."

"No, you don't," Jones disagreed. "But we can think about the open mic night. You or Mads will have to make the flyers and deal with interviewing people, or whatever. I'm not doing it."

"Sure, no problem. But you'll build the stage, right, Teddy?"

Jones shot his eyes at her and then to Mads. Bradley quickly covered her mouth with her hand. Thankfully, it seemed Mads was focused too much on his cleaning that he hadn't heard her.

"Oops, sorry."

"I can build a small stage. We'll start with that. I don't want to do anything too extravagant until we're sure we can pull this off. You get with Mads and figure out the details, then come back to me and we'll see when we can get this thing off the ground. Now, I have to run some errands. Will you two please keep this place from falling apart until I get back?" He headed toward the door.

"Sure, we will. Where are you going? The bookstore?" Bradley asked. She'd been waiting for him to head back there. She didn't want to say anything until she was absolutely certain, and the look on Jones's face told her everything she'd suspected was right. He gave a goofy grin at her question, quickly covering it up with a nod.

"Um, yeah. I need the next book from the series," Jones said. He exited the building.

"So, what do you think? Should we set a limit on people and songs?" Mads asked. Bradley half listened to him, still staring at the door.

"Um, maybe. Hold on." She rushed out of the bar, hoping to find Jones still there. He was, putting his helmet on over his head. She walked over next to him and called out. "She likes daisies."

"What?" he called above the sound of his bike being started.

"Vanessa, she likes daisies, and she loves chocolate. But don't mess with the fancy chocolate, get her a basic candy bar, and if it has caramel, even better."

"Why are you telling me all of this?" Jones asked.

"You know why," Bradley answered. She watched as Jones's jaw tightened and he swallowed before giving a nod of acknowledgement.

Jones kicked the kickstand of his bike and drove off. Bradley watched as his bike turned a corner and let out a breath.

Vanessa sat in the back of the bookstore, organizing books that had just come in with the latest shipment. She found herself reading the backs of all the different purchases, making mental notes of which books she was going to add to her list of books to read. The list had been growing exponentially since she'd started working here. She was doubtful she'd ever finish it, but it didn't stop her from adding more and more books on her list.

She really did enjoy the bookstore. She could see herself staying her longer than she'd originally planned. For now, she needed to focus on finding herself again. Maybe in a little while she'd look into bigger things like publishing her book. But at the moment, this little bookstore was enough for her.

She was so enthralled with reading one of the book summaries that she hadn't heard the front bell ring. It wasn't until she heard footsteps approaching that she jumped up from the ground and glanced around the shop to find the new customer. As she turned, she saw Jones standing almost right in front of her. She jumped.

"I didn't mean to scare you," he said. He stepped a bit closer to her, placing his free hand out in surrender. Her eyes were drawn to the items in his other hand.

"It's fine. Why are you carrying daisies in a bookstore?"

"Oh." His cheeks flushed. He ducked his head, moving the flowers from one hand to the other and reaching back into his pocket for a candy bar he held out to her.

"These are lovely, thank you." She took the candy bar and the flowers, smelling them. When she looked back up, she saw Jones staring at her intently.

"Um, your sister said you liked daisies and chocolates."

"My sister?" she asked, surprised.

"I'm not really good at the romantic gestures."

"Even though you love romance books?" Vanessa asked, her heart fluttering in her chest.

"Yeah, I—" Jones faltered. "I'm not trying to force anything you aren't ready for or if you're not even interested or—" Before Jones had a moment to finish his mutterings, Vanessa walked up to him, pulled herself up on her tiptoes, and gave him a chaste kiss.

As she pulled back, she saw Jones grinning.

"I'm interested," she whispered. He brushed his fingers over her cheek.

"That's good, because I am too."

Vanessa let out a pleased chuckle. She leaned toward his touch. Never could she have imagined she would be here right now.

"I have to work for a few more hours, but I have lunch in an hour. We could go eat somewhere," Vanessa suggested.

"Yes, I'd like that. I'll be back in an hour." Their hands touched briefly before Jones gave her a nod and left the bookstore.

Vanessa's heart skipped a beat. She walked over around the counter to finish some imputing on the computer. There she saw her phone and a new message from her sister.

It's time for you to be happy again.

The End

Acknowledgments

Thank you to my husband, Braden. Without you and your support I would never have published any of my books.

To my family and friends, I am forever thankful for your unwavering support and constant encouragement.

To my Mema, your heartfelt and encouraging words after reading my first novel gave me validation to keep pursuing my dream.

To my betas, Emory and Laurel, my story would not exist without either of you. I appreciate the time and effort you both take reading and examining my early drafts to help me bring it to the next level. Thank you.

To my editors, Makenna Albert of On the Same Page and Emi Janisch of E. Rose books. Makenna, you took my words, delved right in, and did a deep dive to help me fine tune the story and make it the best it could be. Thank you. And Emi, thank you for polishing my final manuscript to make it ready for publication.

To my cover artist, K.B. Barrett, your work always amazes me. Thank you.

And finally to my readers, I appreciate every single one of you.

About the Author

A.G. Hawkins is an author, mother of two, and a military wife. She is a former teacher, who holds her Doctorate in Education.

Her hobbies include writing, reading, binge-watching television shows, and going to Disney. She loves spending time with her family, especially when they get to travel together. Her passion has always been to tell stories about healing.

www.ingramcontent.com/pod-product-compliance
Lightning Source LLC
Chambersburg PA
CBHW021147310726
48971CB00002B/518